Lock Down Publications and Ca$h
Presents

STANDING ON HER

BUSINESS

EXIT STRATEGY

Written By

DG SANTANA

First Edition 2025

Printed in the United States of America

This is a work of fiction. Names, characters, places, and incidents either are products of the author's imagination or are used fictitiously. Any similarity to actual events or locales or persons, living or dead, is entirely coincidental.

Lock Down Publications
P.O. Box 944
Stockbridge, GA 30281
www.lockdownpublications.com

Like our page on Facebook: Lock Down Publications
www.facebook.com/lockdownpublications.ldp

Stay Connected with Us!

Text **LOCKDOWN** to 22828 to stay up-to-date with new releases, sneak peaks, contests and more…

Like our page on Facebook:
Lock Down Publications

Join Lock Down Publications/The New Era Reading Group

Visit our website:
www.lockdownpublications.com

Follow us on Instagram:
Lock Down Publications

Email Us: We want to hear from you!

Chapter 1

It was two o'clock at night, and Laney still hadn't managed to get any sleep. She knew she had to be up by 4:30 to meet J-Rock, but she couldn't bring herself to relax. Her anxiety was through the roof. The stakes were as high as ever, and shit was about to get real. Charlotte history was in the making, and she was right in the middle of it all.

"What's the matter?" Zion asked groggily as he walked onto the bedroom balcony behind her, rubbing the cold out of his eyes. He had to be up in a few hours himself, but he was a light sleeper anyway.

"Go back to sleep, babe," Laney encouraged as she turned around and saw her sexy man stumbling toward her. He had on nothing but briefs and Gucci slides, barefoot. "You got a long ass day ahead of you."

"And so do you," he reminded before closing the distance between them, so he could embrace his beautiful wife. The silky robe she wore over her underwear felt so good on his hands. "Nervous about J-Rock coming back, huh?"

Laney wrapped his hands around her body and kept her hands on top of his. They both gripped on her stomach and watched their beautiful backyard view. It was a mini resort, and it soothed her soul tremendously, especially knowing that it belonged to her. It was her peace.

"More like annoyed," she confessed. "Everything about that man makes me cringe. Nine times out of ten, he's going to make the situation even worse than what it is with his fake ass principles. He moves off of emotion like a bitch but supposed to be the hardest nigga around. Fuck out of here!"

Zion gripped her a little tighter and took a deep breath before he spoke. "I got to have a talk with that nigga face-to-face."

Laney turned around, so she was leaning on the balcony rail and facing him. "Nooo! Please just stay as far away from that man as possible! Let me handle him. I don't need y'all bumping heads at all."

"You know what? I'll fall back for now," Zion decided just then. "Shit's real heated right now with the BBG situation, and he's probably not even in his right mind, so I'll wait until the smoke clears. After that, me and him is going to have to have a serious discussion."

Laney eagerly nodded her agreeance while looking up at him. "Yeah, let all this shit blow by first. We can figure the rest out after the storm," she said before raising herself up, so she could kiss his pink lips.

He picked her up and headed back into their room. "If I'm going back to bed, your lil' ass is going too. We got a few hours of cuddling left."

"Okay, Zaddy," she complied, getting comfortable in his strong embrace. He was her pleasure, and she loved it there.

When they got back in their bed, Laney sucked Zion's dick and put his ass right back to sleep. She laid next to him, in his arms, and managed to squeeze in an hour of sleep before she had to wake up and get ready for the day.

Lester was up and ready with her. Two of her four security guards were waiting in her Sprinter van by five o'clock sharp. "Going to have to give y'all boys a raise. Y'all are very thorough with your job, and I can appreciate that," she stated once she was in the back of the van.

"It's our pleasure," the senior guard responded. "You're one of the best bosses I've had in a while."

Laney started to get comfortable as the vehicle rolled into motion. "You think I can squeeze in a episode of my show before we get there?" she asked Lester, referring to a new Netflix series called *Queen of the South*. She was in the process of propping her iPad up, so she could watch her new favorite show.

"You should get most of it," Lester calculated while reclining his seat. He planned on using the idle time to catch up on some much-needed sleep. He knew how long and tiring the day was going to be.

The ride was smooth. They made it to the meeting location in the north in thirty minutes. Laney didn't get to finish the episode of her show that she started, but she was satisfied. She would finish it on the ride back into the city.

"This nigga got this spot fortified like a bitch," Lester observed as they got to the end of the narrow dirt road that led to the location.

It was an isolated location in the middle of the woods. The closest neighborhood was three miles away. Up until now, nobody in Rock Nation knew about the location but J-Rock and his uncle, who watched the property for him. It was one of the largest pit bull kennels on the East Coast, an early investment of J-Rock's that had grown a soul of its own.

"This shit off the map for real," Laney agreed. "Definitely a good ass hideaway. It doesn't even surprise me that J-Rock's here. It suits him."

"I'm salty that I haven't thought about this yet. We need one of these asap!" Lester encouraged, unable to hide his enthusiasm after noticing it was a dog kennel after they drove through the high, black gates.

It was a whole compound, and dozens of trainers were training different groups of pit bulls to do different things. It looked like a gladiator school for dogs. Every dog was extremely muscled and even more disciplined. The place was highly militant.

"There go them dread heads," Laney said once she spotted two dozen Rastas far off in the open field engaged in a heated game of soccer.

"That's a lot of manpower right there," Lester noted audibly. "And I bet every last one of they ass 'bout crazy as shit. Damn maniacs."

"J-Rock probably get along with them just fine," Laney predicted. "Look at his ass. Nigga done started growing locs," she said before slapping her face in frustration.

Lester laughed as he watched J-Rock walk out of the second building with a carrot top. The sides of his head were faded, and he had two-inch dreads dangling on top. "That nigga been eating good too. Put on some weight since I last seen 'em."

"Shit, Vanya too," Laney chimed. "That bitch was pencil thin when we met. Look at her now."

Lester nodded his approval slowly. "Might need to take us a trip to Jamaica soon. I want some of that food."

"We'll see after all this bullshit." She sighed while mentally preparing herself to deal with J-Rock's presence again.

Chapter 2

J-Rock licked his big lips as Laney made her way toward him with the black pantsuit. She didn't even have a purse, just two iPhones in one hand and a dark purple .380 in the other. She meant business, and he loved that about her the most. She was a woman of her word and stood on all business.

"I see somebody done elevated," he greeted her as she got closer. "You look like Rock Nation royalty."

"You couldn't smooth these grounds out here? Good think I had my Gucci slides in the van. Bitch would've caught hell trying to walk on this rocky ass shit in my heels, nigga!" she spat, purposely ignoring his compliment.

J-Rock stood there with a smirk, very amused with her ferocity. "This a rough place, baby. Ain't nothing smooth about this shit. This a jungle right here. You ain't notice all the lions and bears on your way inside?" he asked confidently.

"I noticed," Lester chimed in. "Might have to leave with a pup if you have some here."

"Hell yeah, big boy! Got some thoroughbreds upstairs in the nursery. Special breeds too. Let me give you a quick lil' tour before everybody else show up for the meeting. Vanya, take Laney into the living space until everybody else show up," he instructed before walking off with an arm around Lester.

"Wassup, bitch? See you sticking beside that psychopath," Laney said to Vanya as a form of greeting.

Vanya's face twisted up. "That's my husband you're talking about. Watch your mouth before I swell it up," she threatened seriously with her chest out.

Laney chuckled as she did a quick visual scan of Vanya. She had on army fatigue spandex biker shorts with a sports bra to match. Her sneakers were tied extra tight. She'd obviously been working out. "By the looks of it, J-Rock been swelling yo shit up," Laney pointed out tauntingly.

"He would never!" Vanya spat matter-of-factly as she took two steps closer. "I been training with my trainer. Got to be ready just in case a lil' bitch think about putting their hands on me again!" she challenged before taking one more step closer.

"Bitch, if you take another step, your husband gone be one hurt nigga today!" Laney promised after quickly training her gun on Vanya's torso. "I don't care how much Jet Li shit you know. You ain't dodging no damn bullet. I got hallows in this muthafucka too. Please call my bluff today. I'm pregnant and will not be fighting during the duration of this pregnancy." She had finality in her tone and fearlessness in her eyes.

Vanya wanted to call her bluff and get her lick back, but she would wait it out. She had bigger things to worry about at the moment anyway. "Let me show you this damn room," she decided with much reluctance.

"That would be nice," Laney responded with sarcastic niceness before following Vanya and actually admiring her figure. Her trifling ass was fine as hell. You couldn't take that from her if you wanted to.

****

Murk and Glock showed up to The Jungle not too long after Laney, and Ice showed up about twenty minutes after them. Once everybody was there, they were led into the lower level where J-Rock waited for them patiently. The place was weird looking, like something out of a scary movie.

The specific staircase they took led them to a regularly furnished bedroom, but they were told to go inside of the closet where there was a narrow, steel wraparound staircase that took them to a cave. The floor was dirt, but the wall looked like it was made of stone, and there was a large pool of water that was almost big enough to be called a lake. When you looked to the left, there was just a solid twenty-foot stone wall from ceiling to floor. A large boat was parked at the steel deck to the far end.

"Yeahhhh, this part of the land don't even come on the blueprints. The previous owner had to show me how to get down here," J-Rock boasted enthusiastically. He was comfortably dressed in gym shorts, Gucci sandals, and a tank top. An army fatigue printed Glock was in his right hand.

He always got off on unusual shit like this. There were other hidden hideaways on the property, but that was the only one he was willing to reveal. None of the others said a word. They were all busy looking around at the gloomy features of the place. He had it lit with stadium lights, so they could see good in there. It was actually kind of beautiful in a grim way.

"Come on! Come on! Let's get this meeting started though," said J-Rock as he waved them to follow him past the other door he stood in front of.

It was a cave room made of stone, about the size of a QT gas station store. A single office desk was in one corner, an LED lamp in another corner, and three subdued hostages in another.

"Who you got right there?" Murk asked curiously and casually. This was normal business for him.

J-Rock chuckled audibly. "Them gangstas y'all seen out there in the field got active as soon as they feet touched US soil. Had them snatch up Tory's auntie, Choppa's mama, and that bitch Tory been driving around with."

All three women let out muffled cries for help and squirmed in attempts to get out of their bondages, but it was impossible. J-Rock was the one who taught Murk how to tie a muthafucka up properly. If J-Rock tied you up, you had a better chance of getting out of a snake pit.

"Woah, since when we started involving innocent women in our business?" Murk asked curiously. "You pulling some lowdown shit like this right here again?" The disappointment was clear in his voice because J-Rock was the one that taught him not to involve innocents. It was one of the things he admired the most about J-Rock. He promised to never harm another innocent life after he put that baby in the oven back in the day.

J-Rock knew that; that was why he wasn't fazed by Murk's tone. "Calm down, nigga. I said you not supposed to hurt innocents, and as you can see, none of these bitches are hurt. They do got to get involved sometimes though for situations such as this."

"What you going to do with them?" Laney asked eagerly. Her heart felt for those women. She even felt bad for Careesha, even though she didn't really like her.

"The two old bitches going back with y'all, but this lil' bitch staying right here until I'm done with her," J-Rock answered with an evil smirk that made Laney cringe. "This lil' bitch ain't no civilian. She chose BBG, so she stays with me."

Ice stood there like a statue, open-mouthed. The fact that people were suffering behind a big decision that he made was eating at his conscious. Glock didn't make shit any better either. He kept giving Ice the side-eye.

"I'm ready to get this shit over with, so I can get back to my mission," Glock admitted audibly, making it perfectly clear he didn't want to be there.

"This ain't going to take too long, lil' nigga. You can go back down there to your post matter a fact. Just leave me a good amount of shooters in the city, just in case I need extra boots on the ground," J-Rock stated. "Just got to show this lil' nigga, Tory, who's Daddy."

Glock nodded his satisfaction.

"What you want us to do?" Murk asked seriously. He was ready to get the whole shit over with, so J-Rock could go back where he came from. He sucked energy out of people, and Murk hadn't really noticed until now. He wasn't human at all. That nigga was a demon on Earth. You could feel it when around him. It was hard to explain, but he knew for sure everybody else in that room knew *exactly* what he meant.

J-Rock shook his head, causing his baby dreads to shift a little. "Ain't no rush. I'm gon' make that lil' nigga wish he would've never stood up against this shit. I got three months to spare out here, and I'm going to make sure that nigga don't get a good night of sleep until he sleeping in that dirt."

"So, you want us to fall back or what?" Laney asked for clarity.

"Nobody do shit until I call for it to be done. We're playing chess right now... What you can do is hit your fine ass godmother up and tell her to front us another shipment. Tory bitch ass got all of our inventory.

"Ice! Wassup, white ass nigga?" J-Rock greeted abruptly, causing Ice's stomach to drop into his ass. "You ain't said shit, nigga."

"You know I only speak when needed at meetings, big dawg. I'm here. Just observing," Ice responded coolly.

"You might not be in the trenches with it, but you still a part of this family, so I involve you in everything," J-Rock assured.

Murk and Glock looked back at Ice knowingly, but luckily for Ice, J-Rock didn't catch that.

"Copy that! Just let me know if you need anything or if there's anything I can do," he offered eagerly.

"Yeah, let me know if you need me too. You know where to find me," Laney added.

J-Rock cut the two older ladies loose and dismissed everyone. A few minutes after they were gone, J-Rock stood there, in the same spot, for a whole ten minutes. He was staring at Careesha creepily and silently before finally speaking. "You about to turn into a woman today," he decided with finality.

Careesha sat up on the floor, looking up at him. She returned his stare the entire time, but it wasn't until those words left his mouth that tears began to escape her red eyes.

Chapter 3

Tory laid on the carpeted floor in his mother's apartment. He had sent her out of town immediately after hearing what happened to Choppa's mother. J-Rock wasn't playing fair, and he wasn't surprised. He felt more stuck than anything. He felt helpless for not being able to save his auntie, Choppa's mother, and Careesha. He sent soldiers to raid all of J-Rock's known spots, but every last one of them were abandoned. J-Rock was hidden good and had them with him. That didn't sit well with him.

Tory suppressed a sigh. He was trying so hard not to become discouraged because that was exactly what J-Rock wanted. He had to figure out something though because he had to get Careesha back. He felt like it was his fault she was kidnapped since she was on a personal run for him during the time of her abduction.

His Galaxy vibrated next to him, causing him to jump a little. He was so zoned out that it startled him a little. He grabbed the phone off the floor and put it to his ear after answering. "Please tell me you got some type of good news, bruh," he begged Choppa. He was sick of the bad reports coming in.

"Laney dropped Mom Dukes off and Auntie off and promised that they wasn't harmed. Not a scratch on her," Choppa informed with much relief. Tory felt his relief through the phone.

"Where Careesha?" he asked suddenly with a boost of hope. "She with y'all?"

"Hell nah, gang," Choppa informed sadly. "Mom Dukes said that J-Rock said he was going to keep Careesha for choosing sides."

"Fuckkk, man!" Tory spat sharply. "That bitch ass nigga trying hard to draw me out and beg him for mercy. He trying to break a nigga."

Choppa sighed. "Hope he don't break her too bad. She good peoples, bruh. We gots to get her back, man."

"I knowwwwwww, bruh! Shit got me at a standstill because I don't know what the fuck to do for her."

"Ain't nothing we can do right this second. Just got to protect everybody else," said Choppa. "Speaking of protection, let me drive them to the airport. I'm about to send them to Jersey with your mama."

"Alright, go ahead. I'll have my mama meet them at the airport. It's plenty of room in that house," Tory said before ending the call and getting up off the floor.

He stood up, stretched, and ran a firm hand down his face. "Agggghhhh!" he yelled out before bending down to grab his phone and exiting the apartment. He couldn't sit in there any longer.

Luckily for him, he didn't look how he felt. He was plainly dressed in fitted blue designer jeans, a white tank top, and white and blue Air Force 1s that matched the white Kansas City baseball cap he wore backwards. He had on a few white gold BBG chains that started reflecting the sunlight as soon as he stepped out of the building.

The hood was alive as usual with the usual activity going on. He'd been holed up in his building for the last couple of days, so people were happy to see him. He returned the smiles on their faces, but he wasn't happy at all. Sandhurst had become a big ass prison for him. He couldn't leave unless he had a major escort, and he only did that for serious business. He had to get on the offensive quick and let J-Rock know BBG wasn't to be played with.

A yellow and black Yamaha Raptor four-wheeler sped in the distance and slowed down as it approached Tory. It was Nitro, shirtless, on the four-wheeler, and he had on a few BBG chains himself. Only elite BBG members sported the chains, and Nitro had earned his stripes in the hood. Tory didn't like Nitro at first, but now, he was Tory's most reliable lieutenant.

"Was on the way to handle some more business when I seen yo' black ass standing out here... What's the move?" Nitro asked him.

"Might as well go see Lil' Shiesty in the hospital since I'm already out here," Tory decided. His lil' nigga was hanging on like a soldier, and he hadn't been up there to see him yet.

"I was up there the other day," Nitro informed. "He talking and sitting up."

"I heard."

"Want me to come with you?" Nitro offered.

Tory nodded his head yes. "Yeah, I need you to go ahead and get me a whole squad for the trip. Can't take no chances with J-Rock and Murk. They waiting on me to leave this bitch. So, we can't be half stepping."

"Just chill! I got an idea," Nitro assured with an evil smirk.

****

Nitro proved himself valuable once again. He orchestrated a two-way distraction to throw J-Rock's scouts off. Tory knew J-Rock had eyes on Sandhurst, waiting for him to pop his head up for air, but he didn't know where. Nitro orchestrated for two different motorcades to leave out the apartments in different directions to throw their opponents off.

The best part about the two-way distraction was that Tory wasn't in either one of those vehicles. He snuck out of the apartments in the backseat of Nitro's tinted Nissan Altima. It was a lot, but the stakes were high, and Tory couldn't take any chances. He had to protect himself at all costs. They made it to the Atrium Medical Center on their side of town in a matter of minutes.

"What's it looking like?" Tory asked the man he put over Shiesty's security detail while he was out of commission.

The man shrugged his big shoulders. "Just family and friends coming to visit him. No threats."

"Good. I never thought he was the target, just at the wrong place at the wrong time," he stated before knocking on the room door before opening it.

He entered with Nitro right behind him. "Wassup, lil' nigga? You 'bout lucky as hell to still be alive. About one hundred bullets went in that car but only two hit you."

"I already know, bruh," Shiesty responded with more strength in his voice than Tory expected him to have. "It's good to see you, bruh. I heard about the beef with Rock Nation. You took a risk coming here."

"Fuck that! You a damn fool if you thought I wasn't about to come see my lil' soldier," Tory assured confidently, putting a smile on Shiesty's face. "When you get up out of here, I'm going to make you a sergeant. Get you a crew of young niggas and some more weight to move. I'm gone step you up, just like Big Body promised."

"Oh, you heard about that, huh?" Shiesty asked proudly. "We was on the way to handle some type of business for him when some niggas pulled up with ski masks and started blammin' on us!" The anger in his voice surfaced as he recounted that tragic incident.

"It's all good because I been doing a lot of thinking, and all fingers keep pointing back to that bitch ass nigga, Ice. Body had stole some money from the nigga right before that, and he was screaming for blood, but Laney wasn't going for it, but I think he still paid Murk to do his dirty work under the table. That's the only shit that makes sense to me."

"That's that coward shit!" Shiesty spat while struggling to sit up in the hospital bed. He had gotten hit in his chest and thigh.

Nitro rushed over to the bed to assist him. "Woah, take it easy, lil' nigga! That chest wound gone take a lil' time to heal."

"All them niggas got to go!" Shiesty suggested strongly.

"Don't worry about it. Shit's about to get real in the city!" Tory promised with an evil smirk. Shiesty didn't even know about the blitz he had just sent.

Chapter 4

The two motorcades that left Sandhurst earlier that day as decoys ended up cruising around the whole city aimlessly. Each motorcade took their own routes for hours, but when they were sure they weren't followed, both motorcades met up in an abandoned parking lot of an old strip mall on the north side of town.

Choppa was in attendance and orchestrated the whole move for that night. It was just after midnight, and Ice Cold Fun Town had just closed for the night, but little did they know, it wasn't going to get opened in the morning.

Since Ice had moved all his loved ones out of town and disappeared his damn self, Tory decided to draw his ass out. He couldn't get the drop on J-Rock, so he had to take his frustrations out on Ice's bitch ass. Choppa was happy to see the deed through because, in his eyes, this was all Ice's fault. If he would've never had Big Body killed, none of this would've ever happened. Now, his ass had to suffer.

"Y'all know what to do!" Choppa barked loudly, so the whole parking lot could hear. "Let's do it!"

The next thing you knew, a mob of forty-six people ran across the street with hoods and masks on. It was destruction time, and everybody was hyped about it. Those were hard times for BBG, so most of them looked forward to taking their stress out on the multi-million-dollar establishment. Once they were on the premises, it didn't take any time to break the large front windows with bricks and bats.

Once the glass was penetrated, a super loud security alarm came on, but they weren't worried. The deed wouldn't take long. One group of people prepared the Molotov cocktails, and another group lit them. They threw the flaming glass bottle into the establishment, and the fire began to spread quickly. After throwing a second round of flaming cocktail bombs into the building, they ran back to their vehicles and took off in about seven different directions. It was a flawless mission.

****

Ice was sound asleep in his new hotel room with a PS4 controller on his chest. He also had his phone on his chest, and he popped up out of his sleep when it began to vibrate nonstop.

"Yeah!" he answered groggily. He was catching up on some much-needed rest, so he was still half sleep at the moment.

"Hi! This is Rebecca Rowser from the Owl Alert Monitoring Company. I'm calling to inform you that the fire department and the authorities are on the way to your establishment on David Cox Road. It appears that there has been a major fire outbreak. Sorry to give you this bad news, but I'm simply doing my job by notifying you on the matter," a Caucasian lady informed calmy and sweetly from the other end of the line.

She probably sounded sweet, but there was nothing sweet about the words that came out of her mouth. "Shit! Alright! Appreciate the notification," he spat before hanging up the call and sitting up on the bed.

He didn't know what to do immediately. He was in so much shock that he just sat there blankly for about thirty seconds before his brain started really working. His shit was on fucking fire! Before he could make a call to anyone, he got another call from the same number.

"Hello," he answered, heavy on the agitation.

"Hi! I'm sorry to bother you again, but I have some more bad news for you. Both of your restaurants and your car wash have all been alerted with severe fire alerts not too long after the first location. The fire department is doing the best they can with their on-call staff. We've also confirmed to the authorities that these are connected arsons. They will be opening their investigation tonight and will be in touch soon."

Ice sighed and ended the call without a word. There was nothing for him to say. He had just gotten fucked with no Vaseline, and there was nothing he could do about it. Tory had made his first move on him, and it was a big one. He was furious and could feel his blood rising.

"Bruh! That pussy ass nigga just burned down *all* of my establishments in one fucking night. That's millions of dollars he costing me with just the Fun Town alone. He has to go! I need him dead!" he spat into the phone once Murk answered.

"Damnnn. That's cold, but it's nothing I can do right this second. J-Rock told everybody to fall back until he say otherwise. I'm on ice right now."

Ice hung up on his ass too and launched his phone at the wall immediately after. It slapped the wall with major force then fell to the ground, completely broken. He couldn't clench his teeth any harder if he wanted to. He was so devastated that he could cry, but he couldn't. He was angrier than anything.

He got up and grabbed his other phone off of the dresser to call his security. "Meet me at the Fun Town. Somebody burned my shit down."

Chapter 5

It was a regular Tuesday night in the city, but the Static Lounge was live as usual. Laney was in attendance since Mary J. Blige was there performing a few of her all-time classic songs. Laney grew up to her music and always admired the way she carried herself like a queen. She looked up to Mary and wouldn't miss that performance for anything.

She lounged around on the floor section with everybody else, like she was an ordinary person. A few random guys tried to hit on her, but she politely turned them down and proceeded to enjoy the vibe in the place. She had a nicely mixed drink in one hand and her phone in the other. Her phone was ringing off the hook, but she had accidentally put it on silent, so she was oblivious to everything that was going on outside of the lounge, but that wouldn't last long.

Mary was up there performing her third song when all hell broke loose. Gunshots and screams could be heard over the music. A dreamy night quickly turned into a whole ass nightmare for Laney. One of her biggest fears had just come to life, and she was shocked at first, but she quickly shook it off and sprang into action.

Some people were on the ground, taking shelter, in fear of getting hit with a stray bullet. Then, you had the people from the front of the lounge running to the back. Bullets flew through the big front window into the lounge, but Laney still made her way to the front door. She got there quickly in a hurried crouch after kicking her heels off and dropping the mixed drink.

"What the fuck you doing?" she asked Dave, who was crouched down by the security booth with his pistol in hand.

He looked at her with wide eyes of fear. He was stuck and couldn't say a word.

"Man, give me that!" she shouted before snatching the gun out of his hand and heading outside the front doors.

She ran outside and was snatched off of her feet immediately by Lester, who was just outside of the door. "What the fuck are you doing?! Get your ass back in there!" he spat after putting her down and pushing her back into the lounge.

It was an ugly scene on the street outside of the lounge. Word had gotten out quickly about BBG burning down all of Ice's establishments, so Murk put extra security on the lounge and a few other known Rock Nation spots because he had a feeling they would try some bullshit. Luckily, he posted up at the lounge because he was able to catch the action. If he wasn't there with the Vultures, shit would've been way worse.

BBG members pulled up three cars deep with intentions on bum-rushing the lounge and evacuating the place before burning it to the ground. The Vultures got in the way of that, so it was just an old-fashioned shootout instead, and unfortunately, those bullets had a few names on them that night.

"Fuckkkk, I'm hit!" Swiss yelled out as he jogged back down the sidewalk toward them. He had run off to chase the cars in hopes of hitting one of the drivers.

Murk immediately went for his brother. "You got hit in yo' stomach?"

"Hell yeah, bruh! Shit hurt like fuck," Swiss confirmed as he eased himself onto the ground while clutching his midsection.

"Damn, I got to take you to the doctor nigga outside the city. Can't take you to no hospital. They gone try to lock you up," Murk decided immediately.

Swiss shook his head with a mean grimace on his face. He was in big pain. "Hell nahhh... I'm not gon' make it. I rather fight a case before I fight the devil. I'm not ready for that shit yet," he confessed as he looked up at Murk with a deadly serious face.

"Aye, y'all got to make moves! Police around the corner!" Lester informed urgently after jogging up to them.

"Fuck, man! Aight, take care of Swiss. He need a medic asap! Hit my line if you need me!" Murk shouted before grabbing Swiss' pistol and jogging off after the rest of his troops. They were parked right down the block.

Lester hopped straight into action and did exactly what Dave was supposed to be doing. "Go inside and see if anybody else got hit and bring them out. I want all the injured outside when the medics pull up," he ordered one of the lounge security guards.

"Alright, y'all! Here come the police! Everybody saw a group of cars attack us before pulling off! Go inside and spread the word," he ordered another security guard that was standing there on stuck.

"Here we go," he said aloud to himself as three police cruisers pulled up right behind the two ambulance trucks.

"We're going to need more ambulance trucks! There's more than two people with gunshot wounds!" Lester shouted to the medic as he made his way toward them.

Of course, the cops were already out of their cruisers, approaching the big, bald man who seemed to be in control.

"What happened out here?" a stocky white cop asked with three more officers in tow, all approaching him cautiously.

Lester puffed his chest out and shot them hard stares. He wasn't really trying to intimidate them but definitely letting them know they were dealing with the real deal. "No disrespect, but me and the manager will sit down with the lead detective that's on the way to take over this case. Our lawyers are on the way, and we would very much want them present before talking to law enforcement."

Two of them looked at each other, shocked by his response, while the other two just stood there staring at him blankly. They had to respect it though. He was so within his rights. He didn't have to talk to them right at that moment.

"But what I will tell y'all is those two men right there are heroes. A lot more people would've been hurt if it weren't for them," he informed, referring to Swiss and one of the lounge's security guards.

"They work security here?" one of the officers asked.

"The bigger guy does. The other light skinned man is a civilian, but he stepped up to protect his peers," he informed sincerely before walking away from them, back toward the front door, to check on Laney.

****

After all the wounded people were rushed to the hospital, the police took over the show. All of the civilians were able to leave, but the detectives questioned the staff. Laney played the angry victim, demanding them to go do their jobs. She made sure to mention Swiss' heroism and told them he saved a lot of lives that night by holding off the savages. He was going to need all the help he could get.

After dodging the news reporters, Laney hopped in her Sprinter van. There was an emergency meeting at one of Murk's spots on the eastside of town, and she was the last one to show up. She had to wait for her and Craig's office to be cleaned out before leaving. She didn't want any valuables at the lounge since it would be a crime scene for a little while.

"About time your lil' ass joined us!" J-Rock said from the TV that was mounted on the wall in the dining room.

25

A phone sat at the head of the table, facing everyone sitting around it, and the feed was streamed to the television. Laney took a seat at the table with Murk, Ice, and Glock. Their eyes lingered on her. She still had on her white mini skirt and heels. She didn't have time to change. Her baby bump showed, but she was still sexy as ever.

"I thought you headed back down south, lil' nigga?" she asked Glock, purposely ignoring J-Rock.

"Day after tomorrow. Sister's funeral tomorrow," Glock informed sadly.

"Oh, yeah, I never got a chance to tell you how sorry I am for that loss," J-Rock said sincerely. "I'm glad you handled that business that can't get spoken on. Proud of you, lil' nigga."

Glock nodded his respect but didn't respond verbally.

"Alright! Let's get down to the nitty-gritty," said J-Rock as he stood up from his chair at the table and stepped back, so they could see him. He hated to talk in meetings while sitting down. "That nigga, Tory, did some damage tonight. I ain't even going to lie. Glad none of y'all got hurt though." J-Rock was sincere with what he said, and they knew it. But it was only because they ran his empire.

"Tory has to die. End of story," Laney stated with finality. "Fuck all that playing."

"I'm with her," Ice quickly agreed. "He just did me dirtyyyy, bruh!" The pain was clear in his voice. Everyone knew how important his growing legal empire was to him, and Tory used that to his advantage.

"So, what we going to do, big dawg?" Murk asked while looking at J-Rock on the TV screen.

J-Rock replanted his feet and folded his arms. "I understand where y'all coming from, but I want that nigga alive, man. Y'all don't understand. I gave that nigga *everything* and trusted him like a brother. For him to say fuck me is insane. I got to make him suffer. He don't deserve a quick death, bruh."

"So, what you want us to do? Just sit back while this nigga burn the city down? This shit ain't a good look and bad for business. You got to use your head. Focus on what matters because, at this point, Tory's suffering going to make Rock Nation suffer, especially if we can't pay the plug back on time. Them bosses back in Columbia don't give a fuck how close I am to Karmen. They don't play about they money."

J-Rock stood there with a serious face. His arms were still folded and feet still planted widely. "Alright, man. Fuck it. Kill him! Full court press, Murk!"

Chapter 6

Laney had fell asleep on her way home, so she was very groggy by the time she walked in her bedroom. It was almost four o'clock in the morning, but Zion was wide awake, like he didn't get any sleep. "I should slap the fuck out of you," he spat as soon as she stepped through the threshold.

"Whatttt, babe? I texted you and told you I had an emergency meeting after I was done at the lounge. What's the problem?"

He waved her over to the bed while tapping his phone screen. When she made it to the bed, he handed her the phone. She grabbed the phone and turned it over, so she could see the screen. She began looking at the video with a squint, then her eyes widened when she noticed herself. Someone in the crowd at the lounge recorded her stalking to the front doors and yelling at Dave before snatching the pistol out of his hand and disappearing outside the front doors.

"Female owner of Static Lounge holds down her fort!" he said aloud, reciting the caption for the post.

It was loaded onto Facebook three hours ago and already had over 200,000 views. This wasn't good for Laney's image. It was going to bring her unwanted attention. The prospective of the video actually made her look gangster.

"What the fuck was you thinking? Fuck you paying security all that muthafuckin' money for? Not only are you the boss lady, you pregnant with our child! You done lost your mind, girl? Let me know right now cause I'm genuinely confused!" he spat angrily, disappointment clear in his tone.

Laney just dropped her head and shook it. She couldn't even defend her actions. "I'm not even gon' lie, babe... I wasn't really thinking at all. I just reacted, and I was mad at Dave. Lester pushed me back inside though. I wasn't in the actual shootout."

"You could've been though! You could've ran out there and got hit right in the stomach with a bullet. Then what?" Zion spat.

She immediately thought about Swiss getting shot in his stomach and how that same bullet could've been for her, but she didn't dare say it out loud. "I'm sorry, baby. It's just been a lot going on, and I guess I been frustrated. Like, I've noticed my temper is way shorter than usual."

He nodded in agreeance. "Yeah, I noticed that too. Just never spoke on it... Something got to give though because you not about to be putting yourself and my child at risk. That's just not about to happen. Do I need to quit this boxing shit to keep an eye on you?"

"Come on now." She gave him a knowing look. "Don't be stupid. I promised you all this shit will be over soon, and I meant that. Just give me some time to piece everything together. I got something up my sleeve, but I have to be careful how I make my moves these days."

He pulled her down onto him and wrapped his arms around her. "I can't lose you, girl. You hear me? You and that baby mean the world to me."

"And you're everything to us, babe," she assured while hugging his head. "Don't worry, baby. All this will be over with soon."

She kissed him then got up to take a shower, so she could get back in bed with him.

****

Karmen arrived at Laney's house a few hours after she got in bed with Zion. When she woke up, Karmen was in her bed, and Zion was gone. It was nine o'clock in the morning, and Laney felt like she'd only been sleep for one hour instead of four. "Zion's gone?"

"Yes, he is," Karmen answered while sitting there with a button-down shirt dress on, chewing on a piece of fried sausage. "Made him a light little breakfast before he left... That man loves you like my second husband loved me. He's a keeper."

"I knowwwww!" Laney agreed as she displayed a deep stretch. "I have to get out this street lifestyle. Been done gave that man a damn heart attack."

"We're going to have to get J-Rock out of the way first."

Laney sighed. "At this point, I'm about ready to do the deed myself."

"Nope! Keep plotting how you been doing. Just let me know what you need from me and when you need it," Karmen instructed seriously. J-Rock was on the top of her personal shit list at this point.

"I will."

Karmen stayed with Laney and kept her company for the day. They bonded as usual and enjoyed each other's presence. They were downstairs, talking decorations, when Mini surprised Laney with a call on FaceTime.

"Heyyyyyy, Mommy!" Mini screamed exaggeratedly.

"Heyyyy, lil girl! I miss you *sooooo* much! I got a few surprises for you when you come back," Laney informed sneakily.

Mini rolled her eyes. "You forever trying to surprise somebody... I'll be back in three weeks though."

"Okay, baby. Well, guess what? I have your new grandma right here with me. Talk to her," Laney said before passing the phone to Karmen.

While Karmen was on the phone making Mini laugh, Laney sat there on a moving box with a straight face. Her mind was in overdrive, trying to calculate everything. She had to make sure the city was safe for Mini to come home to and make sure she would be able to focus on her family one hundred percent. She had three weeks to get her shit together, and she had to prepare for the challenge. Her family was her motivation.

Chapter 7

A black SUV pulled up to the front of Sandhurst and tossed a body out of the car onto the grass out front. It was a woman. It was Careesha, and Tory was notified as soon as she was found. He shot out of his apartment, out of his building, and through the projects. He was huffing and puffing by the time he made it to the front of the apartments, but he kept running once he saw Careesha on the ground with a small crowd of people surrounding her.

"Why the fuck y'all ain't cut that shit off of her? Just got her laying there like a damn fish!" Tory spat before he pulled a pocketknife from his pocket and cut off the zip ties from her wrists and ankles.

"Shit, look at her! She look dead to me. Didn't want to touch her, bruh," one of the young BBG boys said understandably. "We just made sure you was notified, big dawg."

Tory put the side of his head to her chest and felt a heartbeat. Then, he checked her mouth. "She's breathing. Probably got her under some type of sedative. Call the ambulance. She might need some medical assistance. I don't want to take no chances with that nigga, J-Rock."

The ambulance got there in a few short minutes, and Tory got in with her without thinking about repercussions. Six cars, filled with BBG members, followed behind the ambulance for Tory's safety. They weren't playing about their general. They had already lost Big Body, and that was enough. They were prepared to protect Tory at *any* costs.

Fortunately, they all made it safely to the hospital. Careesha was admitted, and Tory waited in the room with her once the doctor was done with her. On his way out, the doctor assured Tory that she would find consciousness soon, but they had to keep her for tests because they found proof of forced entry on top of the bruises on her body.

It was a whole thing. Two police detectives with the special victim's unit came to question Tory about the story he gave the nurses. He told them that she had been kidnapped and dropped back off in front of the apartments. Then, he told them that he didn't see what vehicle dropped her off and didn't have any information for them.

"I'm just concerned about her safety and well-being, but I'm grateful that we have y'all to focus on the crime at hand," was what he told them.

They left their card with him and left.

"What they talking about?" Nitro asked as he walked into Careesha's room.

Tory looked up, surprised to see Nitro had gotten there so fast. "I ain't know you was out there."

"Got over here soon as I heard," Nitro informed as they shook hands. "Got to make sure the king safe, nigga."

"Them niggas ain't out there holding it down?" Tory asked with a spike of anger.

"Yeah! Yeah! They was on point when I came, but you know niggas like me gone keep the structure. We got every exit covered and seven niggas right outside the door. Got all the nurses mad because security couldn't get us off the floor."

"I wish they would. They know wassup with us," Tory boasted.

"Exactly," Nitro agreed before looking over at Careesha. "She good?"

"Sick ass nigga beat and raped her, then put her to sleep with some type of tranquilizer, and dropped her off in front of Sandhurst... That nigga got to die, bruh," Tory spat fiercely.

Nitro grabbed his fro with a cringy face. He didn't like the thought of it. "That nigga is fucked up in the head for real. I done heard so much fucked up shit about the nigga; I'm not even surprised though."

"Me neither. I'm just blowed Careesha got caught up in this shit," Tory confessed. "Only if her lil' ass would've listened when I told her to go back to the country."

Nitro chopped it up with Tory for a few more minutes before leaving him alone with Careesha. Once Nitro was gone, Tory sat up in the chair, planted his foot on the floor, put his elbows on his knees, and bowed his head in prayer. He prayed for God to protect all of his loved ones and to forgive him for the hell he was about to bring to Earth.

BBG was on some 300 Spartan shit. And like Leonidas, Tory wasn't backing down from his opponent, and he fully expected to come out on top.

Chapter 8

They had Swiss over at Novant Health Medical Center. Despite the alibi for the shootout at the lounge, he was still handcuffed to the bed. It had nothing to do with the events from the night before but everything to do with the two open cases he had been fighting for the longest. He was on the run for an aggravated assault in the mall parking lot and the head suspect in a murder investigation that had been going on for a year now. With both cases combined, Swiss had been on the run for the better part of two years.

The police detectives in Charlotte weren't blind or deaf. They all had lives outside of their jobs, so they knew what went on in the city. Everybody in Charlotte had at least heard one horror story of the Vultures. They knew exactly who Swiss was and what he represented. They had caught a big fish, and they were acting accordingly. In reality, Swiss was a dangerous ass person, so they had to take extreme precautions.

Murk understood all of that, but they also knew who he was, and he wasn't going for their bullshit. "Y'all about to be standing right here. I'm gon' go in there alone, and I'm consenting to get patted down beforehand. What's the problem?" he asked the two uniformed officers that stood guard outside of Swiss' room door.

"Can't do it, Mister," the pretty, brown skinned female officer informed with shrugged shoulders. "Our captain gave us direct and specific instructions not to let anybody in the room except for medical staff or immediate family."

Murk dropped his head and took a deep breath before picking his head back up and looking at them. "Listen here. That nigga don't got no immediate family. His mama died from an overdose ten years ago. I'm his muthafuckin' family. Now, I waited eight hours for him to get out of surgery. It's five hours after that. Y'all got me fucked up at this point."

"I understand that, sir, but..." the lady tried to say but was cut off by Murk.

"I'm not done talking," Murk spat firmly. "Now, this what I want you to do... Tell your lil' captain that I'm going to make these ten niggas behind me multiply into one hundred, and he ain't going to have no choice but to bring his whole department down here, including himself. Y'all see it wasn't us that was on the bullshit last night so at least take that into consideration. He saved lives last night when y'all wasn't there yet to protect those people. Shit can get complicated, or your captain can consent to a brief visit. I'll wait here while one of y'all go make the call."

The female officer sighed before stepping off a few feet away, so she could send word to her lieutenant for the captain. She was on the phone for a long ten minutes. Six more uniformed officers made it there before then, just in case things went badly, but luckily for everyone involved, the captain consented to a literal five-minute visit for Murk alone.

Murk was searched thoroughly before being granted access into the hospital room. "Fuck you smiling at?" he asked Swiss, who laid there with a smile, looking up at Murk.

"I heard you out there, nigga," Swiss chuckled. "Ain't think you was going to pull it off, but I'm not surprised you did. Yo' ass always making some shit happen."

"It was about to be a whole standoff out there behind you, nigga. You my lil' brother. I wasn't taking no for an answer. How you doing though, bruh?"

Swiss shook his head. "I mean, I'm blessed to be here. The bullet missed all my vital organs, and they didn't have any trouble rearranging my guts. Shit hurt like a muthafucka but could've been way worse. It's all these cases that got me mad. They about to do everything in they power to bury a nigga. I'm going to end up doing some time for that aggravated assault, even if I beat the body. So, I'm just really preparing for that."

Murk shook his head. He was thankful to hear the good news about Swiss' recovery, but it hurt that he was about to be taken away from him. "Damn! Shit fucked up, but you better not let these folks see you with your head down, nigga. You a Vulture! We face whatever headfirst."

"Fuckin' right... Just got to make sure they don't discharge me too soon. I got to heal up before I get to the county. You know them BBG niggas flooding that bitch."

Murk nodded. "I'll see if I can pay the right doctor or nurse to keep you long enough, and I'll see about linking you in with the Hispanics while you inside. They got good numbers in there too."

"Yeah, handle all that... I know them BBG niggas going to want some get back. I know I shot them two niggas in the backseat of that last car. One of them was a headshot. I seen him slumped with my own eyes."

"Shhhhhh!" Murk said with an index finger over his mouth. "If you heard me out there, they probably can hear us in here. Keep that down."

Swiss nodded, and the room door opened. "It's that time," the female officer informed gently.

"You know my number by heart. Call me as soon as you get to the county, so I can load your account up and all that good shit," Murk instructed before leaving out of the room, thanking the female officer and going about his business.

Chapter 9

Karmen had important business out in Miami, but it would have to wait until she got shit sorted out in Charlotte. At first, she stayed out of the business because Laney was a big girl and could clearly handle herself, but Laney had finally asked for her help, and Karmen was eager to help.

She took the trip all the way to J-Rock's hidden compound, just to have a talk with him. He refused to meet her anywhere else, so she made the trip. It was longer and more dramatic than she'd thought, but she didn't complain. It wasn't her first sketchy meeting with an even sketchier person.

She was prepared to make the trip last night because that was when she usually handled her business, but J-Rock insisted that she take the trip during the day. She was beginning to see why as her driver navigated the narrow dirt road that led to J-Rock's compound. It would've been one helluva drive in the pitch-black dark.

After they were granted access into the high security gates that surrounded the property, she admired what she saw. The dogs and their trainers were putting on a show. She took note on the structure of the place. It told her a lot about J-Rock. He was a psychopath for sure, but he wasn't unstable at all. He was levelheaded and obviously organized. That was the most dangerous kind of psychopath of them all.

"Laney told me to wear something comfortable on my feet, and I see why," she stated as she walked the gravel after getting out of the Escalade truck.

"Damn! You look even sexier than the first time I seen you," J-Rock complimented before making a show of licking his lips.

Karmen had on khaki dress shorts, a white spaghetti strap shirt, and brown Chanel sandals — something simple — but her body made just about anything tight fitting look good. "Thanks, and you're growing your hair out."

"Yeah, it'll look better once it gets a lil' longer," he assured while running a hand through the black worm-like dreads on top of his head. He had on camouflage cargo shorts, a tank top, and Nike slides. He was dressed basic his damn self.

"We talking out here? Or you going to invite me inside?" she asked once she made it to him.

"Yeah, I'm going to take you to the bar. We can talk over a drink," he informed. "My killer right here will show your bodyguards to the rest area. They can watch TV while they wait on you."

Karmen agreed to the arrangements and followed J-Rock to the bar inside of that first building. The building was fully remodeled, and she admired the architecture of the place. It was built like a house, warehouse, barn, and strip mall all in one. He gave her a quick tour of the place, and it gave her ideas that she reminded herself to write down.

After the quick tour, he showed her the medium-sized bar last. It had a decent bar size and stock too. Eight tables sat in the room, and two booths were in either corner. Four Jamaicans sat in one booth on the other end of the bar, minding their own business and enjoying their own company.

"What do you like to drink?" J-Rock asked as he slipped behind the bar.

Karmen took a seat on one of the comfy stools. "Anything fruity with tequila in it."

"Coming up!" He made her a quick but nice-looking drink and set it in front of her. He poured himself a Coke with gin afterward.

"This is good," she admitted after taking a sip through the straw.

He nodded his satisfaction. "Glad you like it. Now, let's get down to business... What the fuck you want?" he asked bluntly. His smirk was completely gone.

"It's not about what I want but more-so about what you need," she retorted matter-of-factly while returning his stare from across the bar.

"Keep talking," he encouraged before taking a gulp from his glass. "Tell me what I need."

"You need to go back to Jamaica because you're only making the circumstance worse out here. Let me and Laney handle it," she suggested strongly.

J-Rock shook his head *no*. "I'll leave when lil' Tory is in the ground. Nobody crosses me and lives to tell about it."

"See, you met the nice version of me before," she informed seriously after removing the straw and gulping the rest of her drink down. "This is the version of me that's not about to sit here and go back-and-forth with your ass... Either you leave for Jamaica in the next twenty-four hours or I'll have forty Black Columbians out here in the next seventy-two hours. And I'm not talking about any regular soldiers. These are our special soldiers that have no family and nothing to lose. I'll make every last one of them get Rock Nation tatted on them before sending them to do some shit that'll make Homeland Security come see about your ass. Please call my bluff! I love to show muthafuckas why it's not a good idea to fuck with me."

J-Rock studied her good with his eyes while weighing his options. He didn't know nearly as much as he wanted to know about Karmen, but the information he did gather about her made him respect her gangsta. She had earned her own stripes in the US over the years, and even he wasn't crazy enough to call her bluff on this one. "Alright... I'll leave, but I need your assurance and condition."

"What's that?" she asked curiously.

"I want your word that Tory will die, and I want his head delivered to me in Jamaica. That's a cartel specialty anyway, so that shouldn't be a problem for you."

Karmen took a deep breath and shook her head. "Tory's time is near its end, and I'll have his head delivered to you personally... Do we have a deal?"

"I'll leave for the sake of my empire. I don't want to throw away everything I sacrificed and built," he admitted.

"I'm glad you see things my way. You're sick in the head, but you're not stupid. I'll give you that," she shaded then complimented seriously. "I'll restore the peace and order out here and get everything back on track, so the money can flow how it needs to."

J-Rock reached his hand out. "It's a deal then."

She shook his hand back, then he made them more drinks to celebrate their successful compromise. The mutual respect was there, and that was healthy for business.

Chapter 10

Murk pulled up on Glock solo in Glock City the day after his sister's funeral. Glock was found in the neighborhood doing pull-ups on the monkey bars. He was shirtless with black Under Armour leggings under a pair of matching Under Armour shorts. His braids were pulled back in a ponytail and all. He was really getting it in, and Murk liked that.

"I see you, lil' nigga! Got you a good form right there," he complimented Glock for doing the pull-ups correctly.

Glock was stocky but also a little on the chubby side still, so he was trying to get right. He recently kicked his cocaine habit, so he needed a positive habit. Exercising was beginning to become therapeutic for him, so he was sticking to it.

"This shit light work. I'm starting to like this shit... Smoke me a fat blunt and get in my zone," he said without breaking his stride.

"I already know the feeling. I need to get back on top of my routine. Just been so much shit going on lately," Murk informed as he walked past the Glock Gang members that lounged around as their big homie worked out.

"I feel you. How Swiss holding up?"

Murk shook his head. "Laney cleared him from the shooting, painting him as a hero, and his surgery went good, but he still got cuffs on him for them two cases he was on the run for. Got to get them lawyers together for his ass."

STANDING ON HER BUSINESS 3 | DG SANTANA

Glock jumped down off the monkey bars and took a deep breath. "Damnnn, Swiss! That's my nigga. I know how it feel for your righthand to get jammed up. I was discombobulated like a muthafucka when Ruga had to do his lil' bid," Glock confessed while walking over to the stairs, so he could do declined pushups off of them.

Murk walked with him. "When you heading back to the country?"

"Tomorrow night," Glock answered after getting in pushup position. "I'll leave twenty Glocks for you. I need the rest for this mission. Just in case."

"Cool." Murk nodded, now standing over Glock as he did quick burnout pushups. "Just make sure you don't get caught up out there. Them crackers don't play fair around those parts."

Glock got up and stood, facing Murk. "It's some wicked shit going on down there, and I'm going to stop that shit... Everybody scared of them folks in the swamp, but I got something for they ass. Watch."

"Sure you don't need me to send no Vultures with you?"

Glock shook his head rapidly. "Nah, nigga! You just lost Swiss. You gon' need all yours right now, especially with BBG on the loose... Make sure you send for my Glocks when you need 'em. My young niggas ready to get busy."

"Say less. Make sure you call me if you need anything, lil' bruh," Murk said before reaching his hand out.

They shook hands, and Murk took back off.

"Come here, Mark!" Glock called one of his most feared enforcers.

Mark was bigger and older than Glock by one year, but he was glad to follow in Glock's footsteps. "Wassup, bruh?"

"I'm gon' let you stay back and run the hood while I'm gone," Glock instructed while patting Mark on the chest with his backhand. "Hold the fort down and make sure you on top of *everything*. Keep everybody in line and report to Murk personally. I'm gon' give you his number."

Mark nodded confidently. "You know I'm gon' hold it down. When y'all coming back?"

"It's gon' be a lil' while. Just hold shit down in the meantime, bruh."

Chapter 11

Tory was locked in with Nitro all morning. They had just gone down to the parking garage to smoke weed in Nitro's car. They were putting together a perfect war plan. The whole goal was to see that BBG ended up on top, and Tory could see it happening. He just had to kill Murk.

"We shot his righthand man, and he out of commission. It ain't that many of them muthafuckas. We just got to knock 'em off," Nitro encouraged with confidence.

Tory gave him a knowing look. "Now you know that shit easier said than done. Yeah, we shot Swiss, but he still living to talk about it. He killed one of ours and wounded another. Them niggas is literally trained to kill, hard to kill, and dangerous as fuck. We got to be careful, man."

"No, *you* got to be careful!" Nitro emphasized. "Everybody want your head. After we kill Murk, you gon' have to get with Laney and work something out."

"After we kill Ice too. I really feel like he was the one that did it too."

Nitro nodded his agreement. "I swear I can go for that shit. He got a lot of motive too. Body had just snaked him for all that dummy money too."

Tory looked over at Nitro with wide eyes. "How the fuck you know about that? Nobody was supposed to be on that move!"

"Who you think he sent to do it, nigga?" Nitro asked with a knowing expression etched on his face. "I'm the real muscle out here, bruh. Why you think Body had me on speed dial? These other niggas be flexing. I hold this shit on my back for real."

"Damn, that's crazy. I knew he sent somebody to do that shit but wasn't even thinking about you... It make sense though."

"I wonder if he washed all that money before he died," Nitro thought out loud.

Tory shrugged his shoulders. "Either way, it died with him," Tory lied. "I searched both of his spots myself. Couldn't find no big stashes of cash. He got all his big money in accounts."

"Damn shame..."

Tory nodded slowly. "Speaking of Ice, I want to get at him again. Make it happen," he commanded before opening the passenger's door. "Bout to go back in there with Careesha."

Nitro nodded his head, and Tory walked back to the elevator. He wasn't alone though. Choppa and a few more hittas stood guard outside of Nitro's car. Tory wasn't taking any chances. For all they knew, Murk was in the cut somewhere with a ski mask and a rifle. That was a scary sight, and Tory would be prepared for it if it came.

"Be careful dealing with that nigga so closely," Choppa told him as they waited for the elevator, scanning their surroundings thoroughly.

Tory chuckled. "Man, I don't trust that nigga as far as I can smell him, but he definitely useful as fuck, so I use him."

"Aight, just making sure," Choppa informed as they stepped onto the elevator after the first load of people stepped off.

"Yeah, I'll never let a nigga like him get too close or show him too much."

****

Tory inherited the munchies from the good weed, so he hit up the vending machine on Careesha's floor and bought damn near half of the machine up. Choppa had to help him bring all the snacks and drinks to Careesha's room.

"I hope you got some sour Skittles, nigga," Careesha said weakly as they walked into her room.

Tory almost dropped his food. "You up! How you feeling, girl? Call the nurse, Chop!" he instructed while sitting the snacks in one of the chairs by the window.

Choppa set the food down then went for the nurse.

"I'm fine, just sore and tired," Careesha informed matter-of-factly.

Tory brushed her face gently with the back of his hand. "What he did to you?" he asked seriously.

Two nurses rushed into the room before she could answer. They asked Tory to give them some space before checking all of Careesha's vitals and blood pressure. Careesha was stable for the most part, but they still said they'd send for the doctor to check her out himself. If he gave her the okay, then she'd be discharged from the hospital.

"What he do, Careesha?" he asked again demandingly. She looked up at him with weak eyes. He could tell she was exhausted. Not just physically either. Mentally too. "Don't want to talk about it?"

She shook her head, causing her long box braids to shift in the bed.

"Alright. Just sit tight. I'm going to get you up out of here. I won't let nothing else happen to you in this lifetime."

Chapter 12

Zion caught Laney in the kitchen, preparing dinner, when he came home from the gym. "Ohhhh, shit. What's going on in here?"

"Heyyy, babe! I'm cooking dinner tonight by myself. I told the cooks to chill for the night. I got this," she informed proudly.

He smiled while leaning on the pretty kitchen counter. His gym bag was still strapped across his torso and all. "I'm trying to figure out why you ain't gave me no suga yet," he said, referring to her giving him a greeting kiss.

"Boy, you see me trying to chop up all these peppers," she spat with a playful mug. "You better bring your ass over here."

He smiled and closed the distance between them. "Give me some love, girl," he said before grabbing her face and pulling it closer to his.

They shared a deep and passionate prolonged kiss. "Damn... must be nice, girl!" Ta'Jae teased as she made her way into the kitchen from the other entrance. She was coming from the backyard.

"Damn, I ain't know you had company over here," he said after pulling away from Laney.

Laney nodded. "Yuuup! Go ahead upstairs, shower, and do your thing. I'll call you down when dinner's ready," she instructed.

"Aight," he said before turning around.

"Clean that thang good for me now, lil' baby!" she said teasingly before slapping his ass as he walked away.

He turned around with a serious warning face before exiting the kitchen without another word.

"I don't blame you for wanting to be a housewife. That man is fiyneeee!" Ta'Jae complimented.

"I know he fine. That's the only reason your ass agreed to be here tonight," Laney told her with a knowing look.

Ta'Jae didn't respond verbally, just returned Laney's stare with a sinister smirk of her own.

****

Laney cooked garlic buttered lamb chops with a loaded shrimp salad on the side. All three of them ate together upstairs in the movie theater. They were watching a movie while eating, but after the food was gone, Laney turned on some R&B music. Laney got up and started dancing. Ta'Jae casually joined her. Both of them danced with wine glasses in their hands.

Zion just sat back and watched the show with a pleased smirk on his face. It was at that moment that he realized they kind of had on the same thing. Laney had on a white sundress, and Ta'Jae had on a black one. It was the same exact dress though, and both of them were model worthy.

"You like to watch me dance, huh, baby?" Laney asked as she gyrated her hips to the music.

Zion shot her a knowing look. "Come on now. You know what make Daddy dick hard!" he retorted matter-of-factly.

"What about her? Do she make your dick hard?" she asked him seriously without breaking her stride.

Zion's eyes automatically squinted, not knowing what type of timing Laney was really on. He knew she wasn't a petty type of woman though, so she had to be serious. He just told the truth. "I mean, she probably could. Not even gon' lie."

"Make him hard," Laney told Ta'Jae.

Zion's surprise showed heavy on his face. "Baby, what the fuck you got going on?" He didn't want to see all that coming.

"Just sit back and be smooth. Just go with the flow, babe," she encouraged him authoritatively.

Zion was a little nervous as he watched Ta'Jae confidently strut his way, but of course, it didn't show. He licked his lips as she closed the distance between them.

"Let me sit on that dick," Ta'Jae said before taking a seat on his lap and gyrating her hips seductively. "I can feel that muthafucka through your basketball shorts. Looks like I do make you hard."

Laney walked up and sat in the seat next to them. "Go ahead, girl. Taste it," she encouraged seriously.

Normally, Laney didn't share her main man, but it was different with Zion. He was her fiancé, and they planned on spending eternity together. He'd been extra busy since he got home, and she doubted he had time to get pussy outside of hers, so she decided to surprise him with a sweet little treat. Most bitches weren't secure enough to let their man fuck their friend that stayed right down the block, but Laney was. She was going to make sure he *never* got bored with her.

Zion looked over at her as Ta'Jae pulled his shorts down for him, and she leaned over to give him a wet and sloppy kiss. Neither Laney nor Ta'Jae had on panties. Laney played with her pussy while kissing Zion, and Ta'Jae played with herself while slobbing on his cock.

Zion grabbed Ta'Jae's silk press and pushed her head ever farther down onto his dick, instantly causing her to choke. "Damn, nigga."

"Oh, yeah, he's aggressive as fuck, girl. You got to take that shit," Laney informed then coached.

Ta'Jae was far from a rookie with her head game. The bitch had a mouth on her, and that was why Zion choked her.

She was about to make him cum in two measly minutes, and he wasn't going out like that.

"Bend yo' ass over this seat," he commanded before getting up and getting behind Ta'Jae.

"Aht aht! She need to bend over this way, so she can eat this pussy," Laney said while hiking her dress up and spreading her legs wide on either side of the comfy seat. It was already reclined a little bit, so she only had to recline it a little more to be all the way comfortable.

"Damn, this a sexy ass sight," he admitted audibly while looking back-and-forth between both of their pretty coochies.

"I like long and slow strokes," Ta'Jae informed. "Quickest way to make me cum."

Zion slid inside of Ta'Jae's sweet pussy just as Ta'Jae covered Laney's pussy with her mouth. Satisfied grunts left everyone's mouth as things heated up in the room. The sexual energy in the room was rising, and everybody was focused on their nut.

"Shhhitttt, bitch!" Zion spat before putting one leg up and gripping Ta'Jae's small waist. She wasn't as thick as Laney, but she definitely knew how to work what she had.

Zion was putting it down how he was supposed to because Ta'Jae began to cream on his dick something serious. He slipped in and out of her with ease, and it was getting harder and harder for him to hold his nut. The way her shit felt, he had half the mind to let off his load inside of her, but luckily, he began to think with his big head.

He pulled out and was about to cum on Ta'Jae's ass until Laney stopped him. "Nigga, you better not. Them my babies."

"All yours, baby!" he agreed intensely while reaching out for her.

Laney got out of her seat and on the carpeted floor with Ta'Jae. She grabbed Zion's dick and put it straight in her mouth. She cleaned his dick of Ta'Jae's juices, which didn't taste bad at all, and continued sucking until he released a porn-worthy load of cum in her mouth.

"Woooooooooo!" he yelled as he squeezed the last little drip of cum into her mouth. That session right there was random and exciting. It turned him on so much that Laney was open to doing different shit with him. His love for her had just grown even more than it was before, and he didn't even know that was possible until now.

Laney played with his cum in her mouth for a minute before grabbing Ta'Jae's face and kissing her. She pushed all of the cum into Ta'Jae's mouth, and Ta'Jae pushed it back into Laney's mouth. Laney swallowed the load of cum then opened her mouth wide with her tongue out, so Zion could see it was all gone.

"Y'all bitches nastyyyy," he teased, very pleased with their performance. He felt like the man of the year at the moment.

"That wasn't nothing," Ta'Jae countered matter-of-factly. "If Laney give me more time with your ass, I'll show you nasty," she challenged openly.

"Yeah, bitch! It's time for you to go home, boo-boo. Nasty time over with," Laney spat playfully, but everybody in the room knew she was serious as a trial case.

Ta'Jae rolled her eyes with a smirk. "Okayyy then! I got me a lil' taste. I guess that was enough... Just know y'all can call me *anytime* y'all want to spice shit up a little," she informed before getting up and pulling her dress down. "I'll let myself out. Goodnight, y'all," she said before sliding into her sandals and exiting the theater room.

"Never will we *ever* fuck the same bitch twice so gon' get it out of your head, nigga!" she informed authoritatively while shooting him a death stare.

"Whatttt?!" he asked with both hands up after pulling his shorts up.

"What my ass. Play with this shit if you want," she challenged as she got back up into her seat. "Are you going to watch the rest of this movie with me?"

"What kind of question is that, girl? You know I love spending quality time with my sexy wife," he admitted before taking a seat back in his chair.

He was looking at the screen, but he wasn't paying attention. He was still thinking about the little threesome Laney had just surprised him with. He couldn't get over that.

Now I'm one hundred percent sure I can spend the rest of my life with her ass, he thought to himself.

That was the only reservation he had about getting married. If Laney was willing to fuck a bitch with him every once in a while, then she was a damn keeper. He couldn't ask for a better woman to spend his life with. He was looking forward to spending the rest of his life with her. He just had to get her lil' ass out of the street life first

Chapter 13

Ice had so much anger built up toward BBG as a whole. They were like a poison to the city that just kept spreading. He had half a mind to have the whole Sandhurst Apartment complex blown up with multiple rocket launchers. If there weren't so many innocent women and children involved, he would seriously consider it.

"Israel, I'm not going to lie... It's time for us to find another place to call home because this is just too much," Porsha strongly suggested. "You're choosing to go through this shit. We don't have to go through this shit."

Ice was lying on the hotel bed, in his own thoughts, when Porsha came standing over him. She looked down at him seriously with a worried expression etched on her face.

"We're not leaving, Porsha," he informed with much finality. "This is our home, and we're staying. If you don't feel safe and want to leave, I understand. I'm not going anywhere though."

"When is enough going to be enough? When they kill you or somebody you love? This city is causing us too much pain, and you just insisting on staying. I don't get it."

Ice took a deep breath. "It's not meant for you to get. You won't understand... Just take everybody and leave. My family and your family. Get a house for them somewhere and a house for you."

"I'll relocate our families, but I'm not going anywhere without you, boy! You know better than that!" She had a hand on her hip for emphasis.

Ice sat up and turned toward her. He pulled her closer to him, in between his legs, as he sat on the edge of the bed. "I need you to go with them please. It's too much shit going on out here, and BBG isn't playing fair. I can't take any chances until Tory is dead, and we restore power in the city."

"You keep saying *we* like you're a part of them! I'm your *we*! M.I.A. is your *we*! You have your own empire, Israel. I don't know why you're trying so hard to be a part of theirs. You will never be one of them, and they will never see you as one of them," she spat before storming out of the room.

Ice rested his elbows on his thighs then sighed deeply. He understood where she was coming from, but at the same time, she didn't understand his need to grow and thrive in Charlotte. He didn't feel home anywhere but Charlotte. The air wasn't the same or anything.

"You ready?" Lieutenant Jackson asked as he peeped his head in the bedroom door.

"What?" Ice asked curiously.

"The meeting with Laney and Murk," he reminded.

A flash of recognition showed on Ice's face. He had been so deep in his thoughts that he forgot all about the meeting. "Damn, let me hop in the shower real fast. I'll be ready in a lil' bit," he assured after popping up off of the bed.

****

Ice only had Lieutenant Jackson with him for security at the moment. The rest of the muscle was with Porsha and his family. He had to make sure they weren't vulnerable. He rode in the back of the Escalade truck while Lieutenant Jackson drove.

The meeting was being held at Laney's second office, the massage parlor. A construction company was there doing renovations on the place. Missy took it upon herself to expand on the property. Laney had recently gifted her legal ownership of the establishment. Ice had been familiar with Missy for some time. He'd paid for her services before, and she put him on some other bad bitches that got down and dirty for the money. He didn't find out they worked for Laney until later on down the line.

"Laney in her office?" he asked as he walked into the reception area.

The receptionist nodded her head and motioned for him to head to the back.

"Go ahead and call one of your best up for my boy, Jackson. Give him the VIP treatment," he instructed before making his way down the hall toward Laney's office.

He found Laney in her office with Murk and Lester. Both of them stood, leaning on opposite walls of the office room. "What's all this about?" he asked a little uneasily. The vibe was a little off.

"Sit down," Laney instructed while motioning to one of the chairs on the other side of her desk.

Ice looked at Murk, over to Lester, and back at her. "What's all this shit about?" he asked with more cautiousness than before.

"This is about you, nigga. Sit down," she answered matter-of-factly. Her pretty face was as serious as a burial.

A wave of fear swept over Ice for a second, thinking that maybe Murk double crossed him and outed him for Big Body's unsanctioned murder. It was punishable by death, and he wasn't ready for that just yet.

"What about me?" he asked, keeping his composure — on the outside anyway.

Laney leaned back in her big leather chair and took a deep breath. "When I first met you, I thought you was the Feds. I remember asking myself *why do this nigga want to be all in the street life so badly?* You got niggas that kill to get out the streets, and you went out your way to get in them. But that was before I got to know you a lil' better. You got a taste of this shit and fell in love. You became a part of the streets, but the streets ain't a part of you, bruh. Never will be. You always gon' be a suburb baby. That white collar shit is another world, and you should've stayed in that lane."

Ice was more confused than anything else at the moment. "I'm saying, where all this shit coming from? What I miss?"

"This is me giving you a chance to go live your life and focus on that white collar shit. You got your own empire to run, Ice. Fucking around with this street shit done set you back more than a little bit... I'm giving you your retirement papers right now. I'm gon' give you a chance to correct that mistake you made three years ago when you sold your soul to J-Rock," she stated seriously. It was crystal clear that she wasn't bullshitting around.

Ice's face crumbled in confusion. "So, you telling me J-Rock agreed to let me go? Yeah right!"

"J-Rock went back to Jamaica yesterday. This my show, and I'm running it how I see fit."

Murk nodded. "Yup! This ain't no bullshit, bruh. Look like you gon' make it out this shit clean. A lot of niggas ain't got that luxury and won't never get it," he noted, speaking on himself and all the niggas like him who couldn't function outside of the street life.

Ice chuckled amusingly.

"Still think I'm joking?" Laney asked with a raised brow.

"Nahhh. I see that you're serious. It's just funny because my girl was literally just getting on me about this shit. Wanted me to pack up and leave the city and all. I love my city though and don't plan on going nowhere, but at least this news will make her feel better. Might be that time for a nigga to go fully legit anyway."

Murk chuckled this time. "Oh, she gon' be realll happy then."

Lester couldn't help but to chuckle at Murk's silly assholeness.

"What?" Ice looked back at them, and Murk shrugged. "What he mean by that?" he asked, now facing Laney.

"Banishment is a part of your retirement from Rock Nation. You can't come back to Charlotte. You got to start over somewhere else. A real fresh start."

Ice's eyes were wide with disbelief. "Come on now, boss lady. You know more than anybody, outside of J-Rock, how much I got invested in this city. Don't do me like that. I'll stay out the way, but I can't leave Charlotte."

"You can still oversee your current investments in the city, but you got to get out of the city. It's already decided... You got one week from today."

Ice took a deep breath and looked at her blankly. He felt and looked defeated at the moment. "Alright, man."

"Man, get your ass up out of here, bruh. Go live life and actually enjoy it... Shit could've turned out real different for you, nigga," Murk said firmly while shooting Ice a knowing look.

Ice knew exactly what he was saying too. His head could've easily been on the chopping block, and it could've all been over right then. Murk was basically telling him to be grateful for the second chance. After thinking about it for a few seconds, he had an instant change of mind. He just had to accept it and move on. At least he would have a life to rebuild.

Chapter 14

Sandhurst was having an ordinary project day when a small motorcade of trucks and cars entered the complex. It was war time, and everybody was on high alert, so when they saw the motorcade, muthafuckas got right. Lookouts were sounding off, and soldiers quickly began to spill out of the buildings, ready to hold down their home turf.

The lead car of the motorcade stopped, and Zion stepped out of the back. He was dressed for a training session because he actually had one after that.

"It's just me, y'all! Chill out!" Zion announced authoritatively at the gathering crowds.

Normally, he would've had the motorcade park toward the back of the complex, but judging by the looks of things, they weren't going to make it back there. Knowing his people and how they were, the motorcade would've started getting shot up before they got back there.

Everybody dropped their guards when they saw it was Zion, especially when they saw he only had his camera crew and security with him. He was doing an autobiography on his life and definitely had to get some scenes in his favorite neighborhood growing up. He led the camera crew to the heart of the apartments and let them get some priceless footage of him interacting with his people.

About fifteen minutes had passed, and Zion was shadowboxing with some youngins on the grass field, when Nitro emerged from one of the buildings with a handful of roughnecks behind him. He immediately pulled a teenage girl to the side and told her to tell Zion to shut it down.

The girl had respect for Zion from what her big brothers said about him, but she had fear for Nitro for the same reason. She didn't question Nitro. She just jogged over there and whispered the message into Zion's ear before running back to the sidelines.

"This lil' nigga think he hard now," Zion said to himself as he locked eyes with Nitro from across the field.

Nitro blew him a kiss with a straight face.

"Aye, turn them cameras off for a lil' bit," he told the leader of the camera crew.

"Nah, y'all stay here. This some hood business right here," he told his security after seeing that they tried to follow him.

Zion made his way across the field, toward Nitro, by himself.

"Was you telling me to shut it down or asking?" Zion asked as he reached speaking distance with Nitro.

Nitro motioned for his goons to take a few steps back. "Listen, I'm just the messenger. You know where that call came from."

"Listen here," Zion said as he took two steps closer.

Nitro took one step back. He knew better than to be within arm's reach of Zion. He talked too much shit for that. Wouldn't catch him down bad like he had the lil' homie that night in front of the tent. "I'm listening."

"Tell Tory to meet Laney at Danny's Hibachi down the block from her lounge. She'll be there tonight at eight, and I'd suggest he be there as well."

Nitro laughed. "Now you know he ain't going for that shit right there. Ain't nothing to talk about... Shit done got out of hand now."

"You think shit is out of hand? Not even close... Tell Tory that he better be at that meeting or she going to put two million dollars on his head. He'll be there. He know that's enough money to make a snake, like you, bite him in the back of the head," Zion spat before walking back off toward his people.

Usually, Nitro would've had a witty comeback to shoot while Zion walked away, but he was at a loss for words because Zion wasn't wrong. Tory wouldn't be safe with a two-million-dollar bounty on his head. Nobody in Sandhurst had seen that type of money but Tory. It was a smart move on Laney's behalf. Very smart. It changed the whole game.

****

Later on that night, Tory found his black ass at Danny's Hibachi. It was a good thing that Laney rented the place out for an hour because Tory came with about thirty soldiers. They found seats throughout the establishment as Tory took his seat across from Laney. She sat in the booth patiently while Lester stood patiently behind her.

"I see you cleared the spot out," Tory noted. "Wonder why J-Rock ain't show up himself," he thought aloud while openly scanning the room, making sure J-Rock wasn't there.

Laney shook her head side to side. "J-Rock went back to Jamaica. This my show, nigga," she said matter-of-factly.

"You expect me to believe he went back to Jamaica after all that?" Tory asked suspiciously while adjusting the BBG chain on his neck. "I'm running BBG now, and we going to live by our laws. Fuck that Rock Nation shit."

Laney shrugged. "He is gone, and I don't give a fuck about Rock Nation, but I do care about this city, which is why you sitting your black ass in front of me right now."

"What you want, Laney? You swear you can solve every problem, but some problems can't be solved."

"That's where you're wrong, nigga," she countered with sass. "Every problem can be solved. Some just be more difficult than others... For example, me letting you live is a problem for me, a very difficult problem, but not a problem that can't be solved."

Tory sighed. "J-Rock bitch ass want me dead. After he raped and tortured my bitch. After he let Big Body's death slide. Fuck that nigga!" he spat nastily.

"Yeah, after all that. He wasn't wrong for wanting to investigate first before taking action, but he was dead ass wrong for what he did to Careesha. I'm sorry for that. I tried to save her, but he wasn't having it... Anyways, he only went back to Jamaica so fast because Karmen promised him that she'd see to your death personally."

Tory shot her a suspicious look.

"Don't look at me like that, nigga. If I wanted you dead, I would've let Karmen put that money on your head, but I came up with a bigger plan, and you can be a part of it if we come to an understanding... Right here, right now."

Tory remained quiet as he tossed thoughts and scenarios around in his head. He gave Laney a good look and saw a different woman from back when J-Rock put her in control. He honestly had gained so much respect for her over the months. She'd been tested time and time again, by J-Rock and the streets, but she always managed to weather the storm. That, and the fact that she was a trustworthy person, was the reason he didn't call her bluff and walk out of the restaurant on her ass.

The chef delivered Laney's food personally. He placed an immaculate plate of grilled teriyaki chicken and vegetables over white rice in front of her. Tory took that time to further contemplate his next move because the stakes were high as ever, and he was playing with his life. He knew if Laney dropped that money on his head, it would only be a matter of time before one of his own people took him out.

He wouldn't be safe in his own kingdom, and the same gang he risked his life to guide in their time of need would easily turn on him for that type of money. With all that being said, he had to play it smart and at least hear Laney out. "Run your plan by me one time."

Laney finished chewing the food she had in her mouth. "Okay... You already chose to step up for BBG, and that's cool. You can focus on your empire. I'll supply you with the work you need to feed your people as long as you keep the peace in the streets. Keep the chaos down and the money will flow. That's the deal. You'll be dealing directly with one of Karmen's lieutenants, and you'll basically be taking my spot in the nation."

"How I'm going to take your spot in the nation and be the head of BBG? Make it make sense," he challenged.

She slapped her face out of frustration. "Read between the lines, nigga.... Ain't about to be no more Rock Nation. All the other cities will belong to you. Just change it to BBG Nation or something just to keep the structure in the other cities."

He gave her a knowing look. "Over J-Rock's dead body."

"Exactly," she retorted seriously before taking another bite of the delicious food.

Chapter 15

Glock made it back to Durham safely and drove straight to his new hood out there. To his surprise, people in the neighborhood looked happy to see Glock Gang return. Everybody from old heads to little kids waved at the cars as they cruised through the neighborhood. Glock had left a good impression on them, and it showed.

His first call was to Kelsey to surprise her with the news of his return. She didn't sound too excited over the phone, but he saw the excitement in her eyes when they laid eyes on each other at the church's weekend service.

"I knew yo' ass was cappin' on the phone! You definitely excited to see a young nigga," Glock whispered to her as he walked her way inside of the church lobby.

The service had ended twenty minutes ago, but of course Kelsey was still there helping her father. She was stacking chairs when Glock walked in. "This is the first time I ever seen you alone," she noted aloud in mild shock with a slight pause.

"I'm not by myself," he stated with a slight chuckle before grabbing some chairs to help her. "I got a few with me waiting in the car."

"Of course! They got to protect the *big homie* by any means," she teased.

"If you really pay attention, you'll see that I protect them more than anything. They love me so much because I'm in the field with them. I'll *never* send them to do no shit I wouldn't personally do my damn self. That's the key to my loyalty."

"I can understand that, and it actually makes more sense now that I think about it because I always wondered what made them so overprotective of you," she admitted.

He set a stack of chairs down and openly eyed her up and down. "I ain't gon' lie. You dead ass wrong for wearing that dress to a church service," he teased, referring to her burgundy sundress.

"What's wrong with my dress?" she asked while looking down at herself.

"There's nothing wrong with your dress, darling," Pastor Mack answered as he emerged from the left side hall. "What's supposed to be wrong with it?" he asked Glock sternly.

Glock raised both hands in surrender. "I was just complimenting her, big dawg."

"You two have been a pair lately. Is this a thing?" the pastor asked with his signature directness.

"No! Daddy, you got to stop that mess! I am grown!" she hurriedly answered.

"I rock with your daughter. We not in a relationship, but like she said, she grown. So, even if we was, it wouldn't really concern you, Pops."

Pastor Mack stood to his full height and looked down at Glock with straight conviction. "Well, she's still working right now, son. You'll have to sink your claws in her on your own time."

Glock laughed as he set the last stack of chairs in the corner. "I'm here to see your uptight ass, nigga. Lil' sweet Kelsey was just a plus."

"You are the devil's offspring, son. We have nothing to talk about. I want nothing to do with you. You can run those streets, and I'll just focus on my church."

"It ain't even got to be like that, bruh," Glock informed genuinely. "I'm trying to work with you for the greater good of our people. I realized I can't do it right without you."

The pastor sighed deeply before walking off. "Follow me before I change my mind." He couldn't stand Glock, but he couldn't even turn an evil man's aid down when they were trying to do good.

Glock smiled and winked at Kelsey as he walked off behind her father. The pastor led Glock into his office and plopped down in his chair. "You do know things were perfectly fine before you came along? The change you're trying to bring is farfetched."

Glock's face crumbled. "You call racist oppression, extortion, kidnapping, and rape *perfectly fine?*"

"Oh, things used to be far worse back in the day. I helped get their boots off our necks," the pastor said defensively with much emotion. It was clear that that was a delicate situation for him.

"Nahhh, big dawg. You helped ease the pressure on y'all necks. They're just not pressing down as hard... I'm literally trying to chop the whole fucking leg off. Give these folks some real peace and freedom away from the white folks. They the real devils, but the only thing that'll get us grace with the whites is me taking out them pedophiles in the swamp."

The pastor stared Glock down through squinted eyes. "Answer me this... Why do you care so much? Trying to win my daughter over or what?"

Glock couldn't help but laugh in his face. That was some funny shit there. "With all due respect, man, your daughter is up for grabs, and I got sticky fingers. You might as well chalk that up... but on some real shit, I just got to see this shit through. Everything in my soul is urging me to see this shit through because it's the right thing to do. Ain't too many times I done used my powers for good." He ended with a shrug.

Glock's answer had the pastor lost for words. He just sat there, stroking his salt and pepper beard slowly. "I heard about your little plan to raid the swamp people. That's suicide. Better off climbing a snow mountain with just your socks on."

"Why y'all so scared of those folks? Folks twice as scared of them than the Aryans. I don't get it. They're regular people," Glock added simply.

"No, they're not... Regular people don't kidnap women and kids before raping them and boiling them alive. Regular people don't breed, raise, and train alligators for sport. They're a different species and the worst type of people. That swamp is haunted, and the way it's set up gives them even more of an advantage. Why you think the sheriff agreed to your little deal? Even the law knows better than to raid that swamp. They tried and failed."

Glock shrugged. "I can't bring myself to be scared of them folks, bruh. As long as they bleed like the next muthafucka, they can get they issue. We some real bulls. Don't give a fuck what's in front of you. That shit getting knocked down... I just want to bring you in the fold because I know you got knowledge that a nigga can use. You know shit most folks don't know about this town, and I need that history."

Pastor Mack took a deep breath. "I'll assist you with knowledge and advise you, but that's it. I will not be a part of any wars."

"That's all I need."

Chapter 16

The next day, Laney found herself at Charlotte Douglas International Airport with Tory and Murk. The three of them were on the next thing smoking to Columbia. Karmen's family wanted to meet her new goddaughter that she'd been spending all that money on. Karmen wanted to keep Laney away from her family, but that was not how the cartel worked. *Anybody* who benefited off the cartel had to be brought into the fold and conditioned.

"You still ain't being clear though. What the fuck is a conditioning? I need to know what I'm signing up for," said Tory seriously.

Laney shrugged her shoulders. "Nigga, I don't know. That's just what Karmen told me on the phone. She had a lot going on and didn't have time to explain at the moment."

"Yo' ass don't even know what's going on," Tory stressed. "Them folks could be trying to sacrifice us for all we know. I know how they get down."

"Shut your scary ass up and go with the flow. You ain't got no damn choice, so you might as well just go with the flow," Murk spat then reasoned.

Tory began to take a step in Murk's direction, but Laney put a hand on his chest and stopped him. "Tory, chill! Because he just took the words out of my mouth... This shit is bigger than us. We just got to play our cards right at this point if we want to see it through," she encouraged.

"I'm going to get me a damn pretzel, bruh," he informed stressfully before storming off angrily.

"That lil' nigga need counseling, bruh. Like you really need to get him some help before I put him in a vase," Murk warned seriously while taking a nearby seat and sitting his carry-on between his legs.

Laney crossed her arms and shifted her stance. "You will not harm that man, and he ain't going to do shit to you. The only way this is going to work is if we all work as one unit."

"Mannnn, aight, bruh, but you need to have a long talk with that nigga because that snake shit ain't gon' be accepted. If he not gon' do right, we might as well turn him into ash now."

"Wassup with you and this vase and ash shit?" she asked seriously.

"Because he a shiesty ass nigga and a bullet too good for him. If I ever get the chance, I'm gon' burn that nigga alive."

Laney looked off and shook her head. "Yeah, you got real problems, nigga. You need to seek therapy when we get back."

Murk didn't respond. He just made a face, brushing her off, before putting his wireless headphones into his ears. They had another hour to wait for the plane, and he wanted to pass time.

****

They boarded the Delta flight on time. All three of them flew first class, courtesy of Karmen. They were originally supposed to fly on the private jet with Karmen, but she changed her mind about it and booked them first class tickets instead. Pictures of all three of them boarding an international private flight together would be ammo for the Feds. They weren't going to hand it to them like that, so they played it smart.

None of them had complaints about the flight. The luxury and customer service were all the way on point. It took them about six hours and twenty minutes to land at El Dorado International Airport in Bogotá, Columbia. It was the most populated city in Columbia and the home to the Port Clan Cartel, the richest and most ruthless cartel in all of Columbia.

Karmen grew up in the cartel and earned her stripes as one of the few respected women in their world. Most women didn't have the balls to pull off some of the crazy shit Karmen had done, especially not at the young age she started at. Nobody could tame her when she was in her young and reckless stage, but nobody could have her killed because her grandfather wouldn't have it. He protected her for many years, but once he had a heart attack and died, her uncle took over and sent her to the United States to handle their business out there. He did that out of fear of her one day taking over the whole cartel.

Four professionally dressed Hispanic men with shades approached them at baggage claim. "Laney?" the tallest and oldest man asked with a slight accent. His English was good though.

"Yes, that's me... You're here to take me to Karmen, right?" she asked sweetly.

The Hispanic man nodded. "We get your bags and carry for you," he assured before bending down and picking up her suitcase.

The other men grabbed Tory and Murk's luggage, and they followed them outside of the airport. None of them were expecting two limousines. Tory and Murk were instructed to get in the first one, and they led Laney to the second limousine parked directly behind it.

"Heyyyy, daughter!" Karmen greeted sweetly with a smile as she took in Laney's flawless African American beauty.

Laney had on jean booty shorts and a graphic crop top with Chanel sandals. It was one of her basic days, but even at her worst, she could run with the best of them. She had a rare natural beauty that made her stand out. It was one of the first things Karmen noticed about her. She wasn't expecting the little girl Armondo told her about to be that adorable and gorgeous.

"Oh, hey, Ma," Laney said as she ducked into the vehicle. "I thought we was about to meet you somewhere."

"Nonsense," said Karmen. "This is your first time in Columbia. I had to meet you at the door."

"What's this all about though?" Laney asked curiously. "I didn't want to press it on the phone because you sounded busy at the moment."

Karmen shot her a serious stare and sighed frustratedly. "My uncle being extra. That's what it's all about... You came up on his radar when I bought the house in your name."

"His radar? What he want with me?" Laney asked with a raised brow.

Karmen fixed her see-through blouse as a slow smile grew on her face. "I usually buy properties using one of our shell companies or one of our businesses. When he seen your name on one of the properties that I signed for, he gave me a call and summoned us both."

"I take it y'all ain't the best of family members."

Karmen laughed this time. "Correct! You're smart. I love that about you, girl... But yeahhh. He hates my guts because I was my grandfather's favorite, and I killed his first love."

"You killed his first love? Why?" Laney asked with interest before crossing her legs for emphasis.

"She got fly at the mouth with me at a pool party one night. I was seventeen, and she was a few years older than me. Anyway, the bitch thought she was hot shit because she had my uncle wrapped around her finger. I had spared her a few times before that, so she thought this shit was sweet. She had caught me on the wrong night and spilled her drink on me..."

Laney's eyes were wide in anticipation, wanting to hear the rest of the juicy story. "Ohhh, shit! What you do after that, girl?"

"Girl, I was sitting down when she spilled the drink on me. She looked down at me, laughed, and kept walking toward the pool."

"Noooo!" Laney chimed in. "She ain't do it like that."

Karmen nodded matter-of-factly. "Oh, yes the fuck she did, girl!" she informed. She spoke perfect English but still had a hint of an accent. It was cute the way she talked.

"So, what you do after that?" Laney pushed, ready for the ending.

"Like I said, she walked off after. I got my lil' ass up and snatched that bitch by her ponytail so hard that she flew back off her feet. When she landed on the ground, I was already on top of her ass. I didn't even think. I just grabbed both sides of her head and started banging it on the stone floor. Before I knew it, the bitch was dead, and her brains were leaking out of her head," Karmen informed seriously.

Laney shook her head. "Mama, yo' ass is crazy. Was that your first time killing somebody?"

"Yup, but I killed four more people that same year. I was out of control as a child."

"Damn, so your uncle got it out for you over a random bitch?" Laney asked disappointedly.

Karmen shook her head in disagreement. "She wasn't random. She'd been around for some years, and she was the only woman he ever allowed himself to actually love. He hated my guts after that because he knew he couldn't kill me for it... Fast forward to now, he's the big boss of the family now and tries to make shit harder on me whenever he gets the chance."

"Hope he don't try to kill me out of revenge," Laney exclaimed worriedly. She knew how those big-time cartel types got down.

Karmen gave her a knowing look. "He's not stupid. I promise he's not... Let's just see how it all plays out. I have something up my sleeves."

Chapter 17

About an hour later, they reached the Port Clan family compound on the far north end of Bogotá. The private family compound looked something like Laney's neighborhood — individual mansions with their own acres. There was so much security walking and riding around that you would think the president of Columbia lived there.

"This where you grew up?" Laney asked with wide eyes. She was currently locked in on the Mandarin ducks floating in the big manmade pond.

Karmen nodded her head. "Yeah, but they added and built a lot of shit onto the land since I left. That was seventeen years ago. It was only two big houses and a shitload of land. Building this family compound is probably my uncle's biggest accomplishment."

They were driven up to Diablo's super mansion. It was almost twice the size of all the other houses and had a lake of its own in the backyard. A high concrete wall guarded the mansion, separating it from the rest of the compound. Diablo's mansion was kind of like a compound of its own.

"This is some different type of money right here," Laney complimented before looking at Karmen. "Keep it real. How much is your family really worth?"

"After you reach a few billion and money's steadily coming in, it doesn't even make sense to keep counting. That was years ago… The truly wealthy value power and territory.

No telling how much land they got now to be honest," Karmen answered truthfully.

"You say they like you not a part of the family."

Karmen shrugged. "I'm a part of the family, but I had to fend for myself after my grandfather died and Diablo took over. Every dollar I have in my personal accounts, I earned. They banished me to the U.S., and I made a fortune over there as a middle-woman. He probably would've sent hitmen to kill me a long time ago if I didn't make the family so much damn money."

"Wowwww!" Laney sang. "I can go for all that though. You never talk about your family much, for one, and secondly, you genuinely adopted me and made me your family."

"Now, you get the picture," Karmen applauded with a hint of sarcasm.

Laney caught on and rolled her eyes.

They reached the entrance of Diablo's mini compound within the compound. They stopped in front of the entrance gate for a full two minutes before the gate slid open for them.

They were driven up the long stone driveway where a group of people awaited them, just outside of the thirty-foot double doors in the front of the house. Laney had never seen Diablo in person, or had a description of him, but she spotted him. "That's him right there with the long hair down, huh?"

"How you know?" Karmen asked her with a raised brow. There were five other Columbians standing out there with him.

Laney shrugged her shoulders. "Shittt, I mean, he's the only one with a robe on and boxer briefs showing. Everybody else is fully dressed."

"Yeah, you have a point," Karmen agreed before lighting a Newport cigarette. "Listen... You don't leave my side, okay? This man is overly unpredictable."

Laney nodded before following her out of the limousine.

"Little Karmen!" Diablo shouted with a heavy Spanish accent. He sounded happy to see her. "Still standing tall, I see."

"Diablo," Karmen stated flatly. She didn't have the energy for the fake energy at the moment. "Always and forever."

"And who do we have here?" he asked while walking toward Laney. "This must be the little girl I've been hearing so much about?"

Karmen took two steps forward and one to the side, blocking him off from Laney. "Her name is Laney, and she's under my personal protection, so tread lightly." She held intense eye contact to let him know just how serious she was.

Diablo smiled an evil smile. It wasn't hard to tell that he was the worst type of person. "You got it... Those are her associates?" he asked, looking at Murk and Tory walking up toward them.

"Yeah," Laney answered for herself. "Murk and Tory. They help me run Charlotte."

"What's up, big dawg?" Tory asked.

Murk just nodded with a poker face.

"I like him," Diablo said, looking at Murk. "Follow me into *My Kingdom.*"

"Y'all do not leave my side!" Laney instructed Tory and Murk before following the crowd into the castle of a house.

Diablo's mansion was old school Scarface style, but it was immaculate. He led the entourage straight downstairs to his meeting room. There was a long rectangular table with many seats around it. Everyone began to grab seats.

Diablo took a seat in the biggest chair at the end of the table. Karmen was about to take her seat at the other end of the table, but Diablo stopped her. "Nahhh! Let little Laney sit there. You can grab one of these other seats."

Karmen stopped in her tracks and shot him a death stare. Her teeth were clenched, and her breathing had sped up a little.

"It's okay. Just let him have it," Laney whispered to Karmen after walking up on her. "Don't let him get under your skin."

Karmen released a heavy sigh while gripping Laney's chair tightly. When she was done, she reluctantly walked over to the last seat on the long side of the table next to Laney.

Laney took her seat at the other end of the table and awkwardly rested her hands in her lap. Diablo seemed like the impulsive and unpredictable type. She didn't know what to expect from the nigga.

"Alright... First thing first, these five men right here are my advisors and protectors. They eat, shit, and sleep in the same room as me. They're here to assess the situation at hand."

"What situation is at hand, Diablo?" Karmen asked curiously with a hint of irritation and impatience.

"You bringing them into the fold without going through the ritual," he spat firmly. "If you didn't bring so much money to the table, you'd be dead. Would've been dead if I thought someone else could do your job."

"Yeah, yeah, you won't let me forget that, but like I said, they're under my personal protection, so they shouldn't have to go through the ritual," Karmen countered defiantly, even though she knew she was dead ass wrong.

She knew what was supposed to be done, but she'd been freestyling so much without interference that she didn't think it would be a problem. It made sense to her at that moment though. Diablo finally found somebody Karmen had a heart for, so he wanted to send her a message.

"You know better," one of the advisors told her. "In order for an organization to enjoy the fruits of our labor, they have to go through the ritual and make a sacrifice. They're no different from New York, Miami, Atlanta, Houston, or New Orleans. They're not special just because you favor the girl."

"Like always, he's absolutely correct," Diablo followed up. "Do not toy with me, Karmen. You're already in violation."

Tory shot Laney a wide-eyed look, and Laney shot Karmen the same look. Murk was studying Diablo.

"What's this all about, Ma?" she asked, not even bothering to hide the concern in her voice.

Karmen sighed before turning to her precious goddaughter. "Listen..."

"She ain't let you know the terms and conditions before you signed up," Diablo chimed in tauntingly.

"Shut the fuck up, Diablo!" Karmen shouted with surprising force before turning back to Laney. "A long time ago, my great grandfather made a deal with a very powerful sorcerer as he was building this cartel. He wanted to make sure he was successful on his journey to the top, so he did what he had to do. He sacrificed my great grandmother to the powers that be and made a deal that can't be reversed. We have to make sacrifices every once in a while, so to make things fair, anybody with direct ties to us has to sacrifice as well. Can't enjoy the fruits of the cartel without sacrifice," Karmen informed seriously.

"I told you!" Tory spat half frantically, uneasiness all in his voice.

"Tory, please shut the fuck up!" Laney spat before turning back to Karmen. "Why didn't you tell me this?"

Karmen smiled as she realized something. "Because I never struck the original deal with you. I struck it with J-Rock, so the sacrifice is on him." She was looking at Diablo with a smirk by the time she was finished with that sentence.

"Who the fuck is J-Rock?" Diablo asked with a raised brow.

Laney answered. "That's the man I'm running shit for. He's currently in Jamaica right now though."

"Oh, yeahhh? We need to postpone this meeting and summon him then," Diablo suggested. "One of you four is going to get sacrificed, and nobody's leaving until it happens."

"Well, J-Rock's a sorcerer himself. He'll make for a more powerful sacrifice. You can suck up his powers or some shit, however y'all do it," Laney reasoned strategically. "He won't come here anyway though. He's a very paranoid man, so it'll be hard to touch him, even for a man as powerful as yourself," she informed, playing on Diablo's ego.

Diablo's face twisted up a little. "Then I'll send someone to Jamaica to bring his head back to me," he decided seriously.

"Not that easy," Karmen warned, picking up the manipulation. "He keeps an army around him. He moves like you, Uncle. The man is very, very hard to kill." She took Laney's lead and played on Diablo's ego. She made a mental note to reward Laney for playing that card. It was genius for sure.

"Tell Isabella to get in here right now!" Diablo ordered sternly.

One of his advisors shot up out of their seat and left the room.

"Who's that?" Laney asked.

Karmen rolled her eyes. "My cousin... She's one of the most feared mercenaries in all of Columbia. I don't like the bitch, but I respect her gangster."

A few minutes later, Diablo's advisor was back with a beautiful young lady that looked like she'd fallen directly out of Heaven.

"Damn!" Murk spoke for the first time since being there. That couldn't be the killer they were talking about. She was the most beautiful woman he'd ever laid eyes on. "I know this ain't who y'all was just talking about."

"That's not what you want, Murk," Karmen warned seriously while shaking her head rapidly.

Murk looked at Karmen and back at Isabella. "*Shidddd!*"

Diablo smiled, showing his mouth full of shiny silver teeth. "I told you. I like him."

"Hi to you too, big cousin," Isabella said to Karmen tauntingly. "And hi to you as well, Mr. Murk." She sounded extremely sweet on purpose.

Murk nodded at her with his signature smirk.

"Alright, back down to business," said Diablo after clearing his throat. "Isabella, I have a job for you. A man in Jamaica by the name of J-Rock. I need his head. It's for a sacrifice, so you'll only be getting paid half price, but I'll owe you a favor if you can get the job done."

"If it's for a sacrifice, I'll do it for free. Just pay my cut to him because I'm taking him with me," she informed and instructed before pointing at Murk.

Diablo smiled even wider. "I love that idea. If he makes it back, he deserves a cut."

Chapter 18

Zion was at the local gym, training as usual. His head trainer wanted him to go to a secluded cabin in the Colorado mountains, so he could fully focus on training, but Zion wasn't going for it. God was the only thing that could keep him away from his soon-to-be wife. He had a few more months until the fight, and his trainer just wanted to make sure he was one hundred percent ready, but he didn't know Zion like Zion knew himself. He was going to win that damn fight — distracted or not.

He was messing around with the speed bag when his trainer, Mr. B, walked up to him. "There's a young lady out front claiming to be your daughter. You never told me about a daughter, so I have her waiting out front in the lobby. Young lady has her own security and all."

"What?!" Zion stopped punching the bag and turned to him. "Short, brown skinned with jewelry and piercings everywhere?"

Mr. B nodded his answer.

"What the hell?" Zion said to himself as he walked past Mr. B in a hurry.

Mini wasn't supposed to be back in town for another couple weeks, so Zion was confused when he spotted her in the lobby. She stood up, checking out the trophy shelves and pictures along the wall. Her tall bodyguard lingered at a distance, and her short assistant stood right beside her, looking at the trophies.

"What the hell you doing here, lil' girl?" he asked as he approached her.

"Hey to you too, Daddy!" she greeted sweetly before walking into his embrace and giving him a big hug. "That boy paid me my money back and apologized, so I just wanted to thank you for that personally."

"You're welcome, baby doll," he replied sincerely. "But I know you ain't come all the way out here just to thank me. What's up?"

"Oh, I'm back! We're done filming, and I missed y'all. I missed my city."

Zion gave her a sideways look through squinted eyes. "So, why the hell you tell yo' mama that you was coming back in three weeks?"

"I wanted to surprise her, but she told me she was on a business trip, so I came straight here to see you as soon as I got off the plane."

Zion wanted to go off on her and tell her that she was wrong for pulling that stunt, but he had to remember she was a civilian. Regular people did shit like that. She wasn't aware of Laney's Street crisis and the danger that still lurked in the city at the moment. Well, she knew about the violence that was reported and talked about amongst her friends, but she didn't know how close it was to home.

"You something else, girl," he said lightly. "Well, guess what? She got a surprise for your lil' ass too. Guess you'll get yours before her."

Mini's face turned into pure excitement. She looked like a real-life Barbie doll. "I hope it's that Lamborghini truck I've been asking for."

He shook his head at her spoiled ass.

****

Mini insisted on spectating the rest of Zion's training session. After he was done, they left together in different vehicles. Mini's truck followed Zion's truck all the way to their new home.

Mini didn't know it was their new home yet though. "Where are we?' she asked in interest as they all exited their vehicles in the mansion's driveway.

"This is our new home!" Zion stated excitedly with both arms outstretched to add emphasis on the precious moment.

Mini's mouth dropped to her chest, and her heart dropped to the floor. She was basically breathless. "Nooooo! For reallllll though? Like all jokes aside? Don't play with me, Daddy!"

"That's on my freedom. Eleven whole bedrooms, bought and not rented. This is our shit one hundred percent. You'll raise your kids in this house, and they'll raise their kids here if they want," he informed proudly.

Mini's face crumbled as she began to release uncontrollable sobs. "Oh, my Goddddd!" She hadn't felt that way since she first found out Laney wanted to adopt her officially. It felt unreal. She wouldn't be able to explain the feeling.

Zion walked over to her and hugged her in her moment of happiness. It softened him up seeing her express so much genuine happiness, especially since he knew she deserved it. "You want to see your room? It's the biggest room in the house. Way bigger than ours!" he informed dramatically.

"Yes! Yes! Yes! *Yessss!*" she screamed with rapid excitement while jumping up and down in his arms.

"I got you. Let me give you the whole tour, and I'll show you your room last," he said before guiding her up the steps to the mansion.

Mini was speechless as Zion showcased their new home and showed her all the cool features of the home. He was being dramatic when he told her that her room was bigger than his, but he wasn't lying though. As big as his room was, Mini had the biggest room in the house — the mega-master bedroom.

"Last, but not least... This is your mini apartment. The only room in the spot with a kitchen, bathroom, and a movie theater. We not even going to talk about that muthafuckin' closet!"

Mini was going live on Instagram by then, so she could share this moment with all of her loyal followers and admirers. Her assistant filmed her running into the room while screaming frantically. The room was way more than what she had in her head, and it was fully furnished and stocked. It was literally a whole ass condo inside of a mansion. She showed her followers every inch of her new spot.

"This is the very first room that Laney decorated," Zion admitted. "Our shit not even done yet."

"Damn, I can't even call my mother because she out the country!" Mini thought out loud as she wiped tears from her eyes. "Let me text her on WhatsApp. I'll hit y'all back later on and give y'all an update. Plus, this lady done decorated me a whole content room, so I might give it a spin tonight on my OnlyFans... Talk to y'all later." She blew a kiss at the camera before her assistant turned it off.

"I'm all on live, looking a damn mess," Mini stated. "I should've waited and staged that reaction."

Her assistant, Anastasia, shook her head in disagreement. "You actually were adorable, and that was genuine content. I was reading comments while recording, and you definitely had them emotional with you. You had nine thousand views just now, and I think you literally had half of them crying with you. The type of fanbase you have lasts a lifetime. I don't think you have to stage anything else at this point. Just be you, girl."

"I like her," Zion confessed in a satisfied tone. "I like her for you."

Mini smiled. "Me too. That's my baby."

"Go ahead and get settled. Let me find a room for Anastasia," Zion told Mini before placing a kiss on her forehead.

"Your ass is going into one of the security rooms," he told her bodyguard matter-of-factly. The security personnel had two rooms with multiple bunk beds inside of each.

Once they were gone, Mini got down on her knees in the middle of the hardwood floor and thanked God from the bottom of her spirit for bringing Laney into her life. She didn't stand a chance without Laney and owed her *everything*.

Chapter 19

Glock was known for his fearlessness and his charisma with his followers. Most people didn't give him too much credit for his smarts. Just because he wasn't scared of anything didn't mean that he was stupid though. He knew the dos and don'ts. After a long talk with Pastor Mack, Glock realized that they didn't stand a chance with the swamp people head up. He had to be smart about his approach.

He'd met this tech guy named TJ in downtown Charlotte a little over a year ago while he was out and about. He was a professional drone flyer and an overall tech geek in general, but he had the cool frat kid image. They met randomly in a Foot Locker. Glock didn't usually talk with randoms, but TJ was one of those funny ass white boys that was infatuated with the *thug life.* He spotted Glock and his gang and instantly won them over with his cocky white boy charisma.

They exchanged social medias, but that wasn't Glock's thing, so they barely talked. Glock shot him a text stating that he had a well-paying gig for him, and TJ dropped everything. He was in Durham within hours. Glock gave him the address to the apartments, and TJ pulled up in a rented 2017 Chevy pickup. He hopped out, looking like a cooler and taller version of Brayden off of *Power.* "Glock, my guy!" he greeted excitedly.

Glock met him in front of his apartment building. "What's up, bruh... Long time, no see."

"I been hitting you up on Facebook, bro. You don't respond like that. Been missing out on a ton of that good snow white coochie, brodie," he informed matter-of-factly. "I've been making movies, man."

"Shit get dangerous on my end, bruh. It's war time. Nigga can't do too much partying right this second," Glock admitted truthfully.

TJ removed his baseball fitted cap and shook his head while looking at Glock. "Damn, I wasn't even thinking like that."

"Of course you wasn't." Glock looked toward the bed of the truck that was covered. "What you got in the back?"

"Oh, I got my whole kit!" he answered eagerly, ready to do business with Glock.

"Let's go talk, bruh. You might just be able to help me out in real life," Glock stated before leading the way to his apartment.

TJ locked his truck doors and followed Glock. "So, what you mean when you say *real life*? You got some matrix shit going on out here?"

"Shut up and walk TJ," Glock spat without losing a stride.

They made it inside of Glock's apartment and parked in the living room. Glock still didn't have the place fully furnished, but he did have a sofa and a bed though. Everything else was in bags and boxes — all new stuff he'd bought since he'd been there.

They both sat on separate sides of the sofa. "So, what's up? What you need me to do?" TJ asked eagerly with his hands clasped together.

"This some different type of shit, bruh, so listen carefully and let me finish before you give me your answer."

TJ nodded seriously. He could see in Glock's eyes that he was deadly serious, so he dropped the comedian role for now.

Glock gave him the whole rundown of his current dilemma with the Swamp Bullies. He told TJ about all the women and kids they'd raped, tortured, and eaten over the last decade. He made it clear that they were the worst type of people, that didn't deserve the breath they breathed, before he stressed to him what would have to be done to take them out.

"What the actual fuck?!" TJ stressed with wide eyes of disbelief. "You got to be playing with me right now, dude. That's insane on some many different fucked up levels."

"You need me to take you to the police station, so you can talk to the sheriff about it?" Glock asked seriously.

TJ's eyes grew wider. "The police know about that? Why don't they just handle it?"

"They tried over the years. That swamp is impossible to raid on ground, and they never got any concrete proof on them, so the Feds won't get involved. I need to handle this situation for so many different reasons, but on top of all that, I'm finally doing something for the greater good. My first time doing God's work, and I might need your help doing it."

TJ took a deep breath. "That's some fucked up shit, dude, and I understand where you're coming from. I'll help you with this for free, but my associates are going to have to be paid a pretty penny for this type of job. I know a guy in Montana who's perfect for the job. He's a legend."

"I don't care about the cost. My money's long these days. I just need this job done quickly, correctly, and efficiently," Glock assured seriously.

TJ nodded. "I got you, bro. I promise we'll get this job done."

Glock sat back on the sofa and nodded his satisfaction. He was on to something. TJ just might be able to get him where he needed to be without taking unnecessary losses.\

Chapter 20

Laney woke up in the middle of the night and sat up in the bed. She was in one of the many guest rooms in Diablo's home. She couldn't go to sleep because so much was on her mind — even more than usual — and the fact that she was basically being held hostage didn't help at all.

Murk went to Jamaica with Isabella, but Laney and Tory had to stay until their return. Diablo made it clear that rules had to be followed, and one of them had to take one for the team — to be sacrificed. If Murk and Isabella didn't make it back with J-Rock's head, one of their heads would be removed. It was too much, but Laney tried to think positively. If everything went right in Jamaica, it would be the answer to all of her problems, but if it didn't, it would be a nightmare.

She got up, took a piss, and found her way to Karmen's room. She was snoring peacefully with eye covers on, like she wasn't a psychotic cartel boss. She was a light sleeper though, so when Laney got in the bed with her, she woke up instantly. "Ohhh! It's you," she said once she noticed it was Laney.

"I cannot sleep to save my life. I don't know how you do it... Nigga done took a bitch's phone and everything," she whined miserably as she made herself comfortable under Karmen's blanket.

"Well, if it makes you feel any better, he confiscated my phone too. He's just playing his usual mind games and being power struck. He could've sacrificed six goats instead, but he wants to be evil. He's a very dark man, and I stay far away from him for a reason."

Laney sighed deeply while shaking her head in disgust. "Whole time I'm thinking J-Rock is the worst type of muthafucka there is."

"There's always somebody bigger and badder. He makes J-Rock seem like an innocent civilian," Karmen said matter-of-factly.

"You think they going to get the job done?" Laney asked curiously. "You seen J-Rock's security and paranoia with your own eyes."

"And I've also seen Isabella in action with my own eyes. The bitch is like a little ninja... She'll find a way. Just hope your friend can keep up with her because she's like a cat with nine lives. I've seen her lead a crew of certified sicarios into battle and was the only one to return without a scratch. People in Columbia talk about her like a myth for a reason. The bitch has a gift for death."

"I hope they figure that damn shit out," Laney prayed aloud. "I miss my man and my daughter."

"I'm sure they miss you too." Karmen wrapped an arm around her and pulled her in. "I'm going to make sure you make it back home to them."

Laney didn't respond. She just closed her eyes and took deep breaths until she finally fell asleep in Karmen's arms.

****

"It's sad how you hold grudges over decades like that. We need to put that bullshit behind us. We're supposed to be family," Karmen said to Diablo the next morning.

She found him in his backyard pool, eating a full breakfast on an oversized floaty. It was like an air mattress floating on water.

He had on nothing but a silver speedo with Versace shades on. "I hold no grudge against you. I just deal with you accordingly since you feel like you're above this family and our way of living."

"You just with that old school shit, and I can't get with it," she spat. "I'm a stand-up boss bitch, and I helped build all this. I refuse to be handled by anyone."

"And that's why you're the boss of the gringos," he informed mockingly. "You know the rules. I'm not going to treat this organization any different just because you favor the girl. I've been fair with you lately, so I don't want to hear you bitching." He said that last sentence in Spanish.

Karmen sighed. "When they make it back with J-Rock's head, we're leaving, and I don't want to talk to or see you again. I'll deal with your advisors," she spat angrily in Spanish.

"If they make it back with his head, you mean," he corrected her in English. "If they don't, your little precious daughter will have to choose out of those two dudes who will be sacrificed. Well, that's if the pretty boy makes it back. If he doesn't, then I'll choose out of him and her."

"Like I said, when they make it back, fall the fuck back!" she barked before stomping back into the house.

91

Chapter 21

A few days later, Murk was getting an early morning workout in, preparing himself for the upcoming mission at hand. He had to be in tiptop shape to keep up with Isabella's little energetic ass.

She was definitely *way more* than what met the eye. As deadly as Murk had become, she was easily twice as dangerous. They'd been training in Mexico for the last two days. Isabella took the necessary detour because she had to see how far behind Murk was in combat skills. To her surprise, he was far more advanced than the average street punk. He was lethal and had miles of potential.

He was doing high speed sit ups when she walked up to him. The training facility had a separate full gym. "You think you ready to roll with me? I'm trying to execute this mission in one night. If everything goes as planned, we should be leaving with J-Rock's head before the sun touches the sky," she asked, looking down at him with wondering eyes.

"Got me out here on some *Mission Impossible* ass shit," Murk spat without losing his stride. "Why we can't just snipe his ass from long distance? That's the best route. You trying to complete an impossible mission. Our chances of survival is literally like eighteen percent. It can be done, but we need an army if we want to stand a better chance. At least twenty-five men. I'm telling you. J-Rock is well protected."

"It's only impossible for you because you never seen it done," she stated. "We can't snipe him because we need the actual head. His head must leave from his body. It's the only way for this to work."

Murk did his last ten sit-ups before standing up to face her with both hands on his head, so he could breathe better. "Okay, so we can snipe his ass. Wait for the morgue to come get the body then bust in that muthafucka and chop the head off the body in there."

"That would be a perfect ass plan if the head from a dead body was worth a damn. The heart has to be pumping when my blade touches his neck," she schooled. "Relax, homeboy... Just follow my lead and keep up as best you can. Diablo tried to send me alone for a reason. Most people can't keep up with me, but you have potential. I have faith in you, so those eighteen percent is actually a thirty-five now."

Murk admired her perfect backside as she sashayed away, swinging the silky, thick braid that hung down to her ass. He never saw anyone look that good in camouflage soldier gear.

"Swiss ain't gone believe this shit," he said to himself humorously. "Got me out here with the vampire bitch off *Underworld* and shit."

He walked over to the treadmills and got straight to it. Full speed. It was imperative that he kept up with Isabella. They had a five-mile high speed hike through a rough patch of Jamaican woods by Blue Mountain with limited supplies. He would be able to make it there with no problem, but it was the hike back he was worried about. He knew Isabella would be able to do it without much effort, but he would be giving it all he had, so he had to prepare himself mentally.

"Death is not an option," he whispered to himself as he picked up the speed on the treadmill.

There was a Vulture slogan that they chanted to themselves before heading into battle. All of the hard training he'd been doing over the years was finally about to show at its fullest. He'd never had the chance to test his tactical and survival skills until now. Failure wasn't an option at all, so he just prepared himself. He couldn't remember the last time he'd been nervous like this.

He could hear Ronnie in his ear now. "Fuck that humble shit! You have to believe you're invincible when you're in that field!"

Murk lived by those words, and he hung onto them now more than ever.

Chapter 22

Mini was trying to enjoy a late evening swim in the inside pool, but her mind was racing too much. She'd been home for over forty-eight hours, and she hadn't heard one word from Laney. That wasn't like her at all. She was a slow texter and rarely called, but she *always* checked in. Mini was getting a bad taste in her mouth.

She got out of the pool and wrapped her large towel around herself to cover up the revealing Gucci bikini she wore. After sliding into her Gucci slippers, she made her way into the kitchen where she found Zion enjoying a steak dinner prepared by the cooks.

"Alright, something got to give," Mini stressed as she walked up to the kitchen table. "Mommy never went this damn long without talking to me. Something ain't right. She go on a sudden trip to Columbia, and now she ghost? Nahhhh, I don't like that."

"She aight, baby. Told you she on a spa retreat. They probably turned in their phones, so they can get the whole peaceful experience without worldly distractions... She been working harder than any person I know for *soooo* long. She needed this break. Don't worry. She'll be back," he assured falsely.

Truth was, he was even more worried than Mini was, but he had to keep the hope alive for both of their sanities. Laney was the beat to both of their hearts, and they would be lost without her. God knew that, so he doubted God would do that to him. He still prayed for her safety every thirty minutes.

"Okayyy! I miss her so fucking much. She need to bring her ass home!" She pouted sadly before taking a seat at the table.

"Eat you a plate of this shit," Zion strongly suggested while pointing down at the plate. "Shit so good, it'll make you feel a little better." He waved for them to make her a plate. "It's a nice Friday night out there. Want to step out somewhere? The media would love to see me with my future daughter. I haven't been doing too much partying lately," he suggested thoughtfully.

Mini smiled. "You're probably tired as hell. You don't have to do all that for me. Get your sleep. You have to be at the gym early in the morning. You'll feel like shit in the morning. I wouldn't do that to you."

"I'm not going to drink," he assured. "Just going to kick it with my daughter and get you some publicity to add to your image."

She looked down at her phone and smiled. "It's only eight-thirty, so I could find a spot for tonight. Let me go Live, so I can bring some of my followers. Got to have a fan crowd there."

"I thought your mother was Hollywood," he joked before taking another bite of his steak.

Mini rolled her eyes as she quickly mashed buttons on her phone.

****

They arrived at a local upscale club downtown that was making a name of itself in the city of Charlotte. Mini already had an entourage of cameramen and top fans waiting for her in front of the club. Them, along with the entourage that they pulled up with, turned into a whole vibe. There was even a reporter for a local urban media outlet there to interview them in front of the club before they went in.

"Hi, my name is Jazzy with Charlotte's Hottest Entertainment. Who am I here with tonight? You two look very good together, might I add?" she asked sweetly into her little microphone.

Mini and Zion were mic'd up, so they wouldn't have to hold mics.

"Girl, this is my stepfather, not my man," Mini informed immediately for the record. "I'm Mini Da Baddest, and I already know many of you have seen this man already on your TV screens. He's Zion Da Savage! The future light heavyweight champion of the world. We're just out to have a good time to welcome me back into the city. I've been in Cali, filming for this new show that's about to air on Netflix soon."

"Oh, there's two superstars in the building tonight, huh?" the reporter joked seriously. "How's your mother handling both of your careers?"

That question took Mini for a loop, and she wasn't prepared for it at all, and it showed. She was lost for words and just stared at the reporter blankly.

Zion quickly caught on and jumped in for the save. "She's a busy woman herself with her business and all of her investments. She's also a community role model on top of all of that, so she barely pays attention to the media. She's definitely proud though and wildly supportive."

"That's good to hear... Congratulations on your beautiful family, and I hope y'all enjoy the night. I see all of the people y'all brought out tonight. Y'all are both looking very nice as well."

"Thanks!" he said while looking down at himself with the prayer hands. He had on shiny black Pradas, black jeans, and a sparkling Gucci polo shirt. "I had to make her change a few times," he joked truthfully. "Couldn't be coming out the house with her pops any kind of way."

"You go, Popsss!" Jazzy agreed humorously. "She looks so beautiful too!"

Mini had on one of Laney's business suits, out of her new summer collection, because Zion wouldn't let her wear anything in her own closet. "I guess all dads are the exact same when it comes to their daughters," Mini countered with a playful roll of her eyes.

"Alright, let us get inside of this club, so we can catch this performance," Zion said, cutting the interview short.

He could tell Mini wasn't feeling it anymore. He could tell that question about her mother hit too close.

"You good?" he asked her as he led her toward the club by hand.

"Yeah, I'm good," she assured. "I just hope my mother is good too."

Chapter 23

Tory hadn't been getting much sleep himself lately. Between memories of Big Body, thoughts of Careesha, and his current situation with the cartel, he couldn't find peace at the moment.

Like any other cartel drug lord, Diablo had bricks of pure cocaine on standby just for occasional use. One of Diablo's advisors offered him some the other day, but he turned him down. After a few days had passed, Tory went looking for the guy and bought a fist full of dope from him for only a hundred American dollars. That would've been four times as much in the States. He tried to pay him three hundred more dollars to use his phone for an hour, but he wasn't going for it. After buying the dope, Tory walked straight back to the guest room he'd been holed up in for the past four days.

Laney went out and did little shit with Karmen. They went swimming together, hit the gym together, took walks in the garden maze, but Tory wasn't with all that shit. He didn't trust a single soul there, including Laney, so he wasn't about to fake kick it with them. Diablo wanted him dead and was holding him hostage in a big sexy ass prison without his phone. He was pissed.

The TV was all Hispanic channels he couldn't understand, but they did have a PlayStation 4, so he'd been playing *2K14* and *Call of Duty Black Ops* whenever he wasn't sleeping. Boredom got the best of him on that day though, so there he was, snorting pure coke off of the granite dresser.

"Wooooooo-ssshiiittttt!" he yelled as he stood back up straight and looked into the mirror as the dope drained into his system. It hit him instantly. He stood there, looking at himself through wide eyes, with a slight smirk on his face. He was blitzed off of one little bump. It wasn't his first time snorting cocaine either. He used to do it on a regular basis during his younger years, so he wasn't new to his nose, but that pure shit hit different. He felt like a whole new man.

"Damn!" he said before bending over to take another bump, just to be sure.

"Yuuuuuuupppp! That shit is strong as fuck... If I make it out of this muthafucka alive, I won't cut another brick in my life. Selling nothing but fish scale from now on. Fuck the streets up with this shit like the 80s," he said to himself, referring to uncut dope.

Three hours later, Tory was still standing at the dresser. He was banging on the dresser with his fist to make a beat while he rapped over it. He put his blue Kansas City Royals baseball cap on to the side and changed back into his white and blue Fendi t-shirt. He was feeling himself and passing the hell out of some time. He wasn't even aware he'd been standing there for three hours.

A knock on the door stopped him in his tracks. The only people who knocked on his door were the cooks to deliver his food, but the knock was too hard this time. He knew it was someone else.

"Yooo!" he yelled out.

His door opened, and Diablo casually strolled in there with his open silk robe and briefs underneath. "It's just me," he said in his strong accent, but Tory understood him perfectly.

"Hey, man! I know this your house and all, but you in my room, playa. Gon' cover that shit up, bruh. Your ass don't never wear clothes," Tory spat with deadly seriousness.

"This is my house, and I wear what the fuck I want. I stopped wearing clothes after I became a billionaire," Diablo informed truthfully. He hadn't worn a full set of clothes in years, and that was only for an important funeral.

Tory shook his head. "Whateva."

"What you up to in here?" Diablo asked while eyeing the small pile of coke on the dresser.

"You ain't been in here all this time but want to suddenly pop up when a nigga doing my lil' thang."

Diablo smiled his silver-toothed smile. "Hey, what can I say? I don't trust anyone who doesn't get their nose dirty."

"You're a very weird individual. You know that?" Tory asked sincerely.

He wasn't even trying to be funny, and Diablo could tell. "It comes with the territory. There are no usual men in my line of work, and if there is, they won't last long."

"Bruh, ain't nothing for us to talk about," Tory stressed with a crumbled face. "You the same nigga trying to kill a nigga."

"You wouldn't even be here if Karmen would've mailed me one of your heads months ago. This level of the game comes at a price, and she should've made that clear. She knew this day was coming. Blame her."

Tory took a deep breath and shook his head. "So, If Murk don't make it back, then I'm dead, right?"

"There's a fifty percent chance of that," Diablo answered truthfully before helping himself to a seat on the edge of Tory's bed. "Don't think just because Karmen favors the girl that she won't get picked. Whoever my superior guides me to pick is going to die. Karmen can't stop that, no matter how much she loves the girl."

That made Tory feel better in a fucked-up way, but his life was still on the line, so he wasn't exactly thrilled. "So, what you come up here for? Outside of that, it still ain't nothing for us to talk about."

"I want to hear what you were saying on that song you were rapping."

Tory cocked his head to the side and squinted his eyes. "You been spying on me, nigga?" he asked angrily.

"Of course! How you think I made it this far?" Diablo asked logically.

Tory couldn't even counter that because he was right. He'd probably do the same if he was in Diablo's shoes. "Shit crazy."

"You going to let me hear the song or no?" Diablo asked seriously. "I walked all the way up here from the basement to hear." He crossed his legs for emphasis.

Tory wanted to tear back into him with the weird feminine activity, but he just shook his head instead. Diablo was too far set in his own ways. Nothing he said would make a difference to that man.

He turned around and faced the dresser. *Sniffff!*

"What the hell?!" he said as he turned around. Diablo had just done a large line off of a pocketknife he had tucked in his briefs.

Diablo shrugged. "Just to get in the mood right. I want to feel it. What you saying?"

"Might as well get me one in too, shiddd. Got me in this bitch rapping like I'm in the county again," Tory said before taking another bump. He wasn't ready to do that shit in lines.

After catching the drain, Tory stretched his arms and then dropped the beat on the dresser. He just hit the beat for a little while, so he could catch the feel of it.

My brother, he gone as fuck!
Damn!
Can't wait to catch up with his killer!
Wrong or right,
I'mma be a real nigga!
I'mma make all da real niggas feel me!
Shit get different!
I feel different!

She suspicious!
He suspicious!
Shit ridiculous!
How did I miss it?
On the dope, but pain ain't healin!

"I got to make sure he rest, but that's how that shit go," Tory informed after turning back around to face Diablo.

Diablo sat there, nodding his sincere approval. Tory had good rhythm on that song, and most of all, you could literally feel all the pain in his words. They came from his soul, and Diablo felt it. "I know what you say in the rap is true, how you feel. Just know, whatever happens here, I have a respect for you," he said before standing and walking up to shake Tory's hand.

Tory shook his hand without a word and watched as the drug lord left his room. He didn't know how to feel about that last statement, but he was glad that Diablo liked and felt his song.

"Might as well finish this muthafucka. Ain't got shit else going on," he said to himself before pounding his fist on the dresser once more.

On the dope, but pain ain't healin!
Swear, I can't explain this feelin'!
At the plug's house, thinkin' 'bout Careesha...
Is she healing?

Chapter 24

Isabella had connections that reached all the way to Jamaica. Her family's money came with a lot of connections, and it was all at her disposal. Whatever resources were needed to get the job done were available to her. They flew undetected into Jamaica in the back of a government cargo plane. They arrived at the top of the evening.

The only equipment they had was in the big duffle bags they carried. "So, what's next?" Murk asked curiously.

The fact that he was anxious fucked with his pride. He prided himself on staying calm during storms, so the fact that he was genuinely nervous was a problem for him. Isabella being unbothered, like a butterfly on a hot summer day, didn't help either.

"We're about to get into this car and head to the forest. We have a tough ass hike ahead of us. I seen the layout of these woods on a satellite, and judging from my expertise, we going to have to push it to make it there and back on time," she answered as they walked toward the grey 2003 Honda with tinted windows.

"You think we going to run into twelve on our way?" he asked, trying to plan for the scenario in his head.

She stopped in her tracks and gave him a weird look. "Are you referring to the police?"

"Yeah... My bad. That's some American shit," he apologized amusingly.

She shook her head. "I'm hip to American lingo, but I just don't understand that. Why do you refer to the police as the number twelve?" she asked with genuine curiosity.

Murk looked around with a weird look now on his own face. "Shiddd, now that you ask... I don't even know!" he answered truthfully after raking his brain for a moment. "Damn, I never even thought of it. I don't even know, bruh."

"That's sad," she informed disappointedly as she started back walking to the car. "Might want to get you some rest, baby boy. Thirty-minute drive to our checkpoint," she teased as they got into the car.

Murk tossed his duffle bag in the backseat before hopping into the passenger's seat. "Just drive the damn car. You won't have to worry about me. I'm trained for this shit," he spat with a little more confidence than he really had.

"You're so cute," she teased before bringing the car's engine to life.

****

They reached their checkpoint a little behind schedule, but they still made some good time. Isabella parked the car in a nice little blind spot that she had to be told about because most people would miss the turn to the road they took. They were officially in the field, and it was official go-time.

"Come on!" Isabella instructed as she began to grab accessories out of her duffle. "The sun will be setting in about an hour or so. The plan is to be at least two miles into the hike by the time the sun disappears."

They were behind the car, using the trunk for a table to get their equipment ready. Isabella did a full check on her guns and filled all her holsters up with different gadgets that she'd found useful over the years.

"Alright, I'm ready," Murk informed with surprising enthusiasm. He had found his motivation. His mind was ready for the mission ahead. "What's up with all this extra shit you packed in these bags?"

"It's called a survival kit. We're going to take it with us, but we're going to stash the bags about a mile out from the compound, just in case we get stuck in the forest. We'll have what we need to survive out here for a few days while we hide," she informed comfortably.

Murk stared at her blankly. "You should've joined the damn military."

She rolled her eyes with exaggeration. "The military doesn't pay seven figures for jobs. My family does."

"You got a point right there," he agreed before throwing his duffle over his back, so he could tote it. "Let's do it."

She did the same with her duffle, and they were on their way. The mission had officially begun.

"Keep up, cutie!" she challenged before breaking into a paced jog through the trees.

Murk took a deep ass breath and followed suit. He was determined to see the whole mission through.

Chapter 25

Glock tried to call Murk a few times to check in and ask for a little tactical advice for his upcoming visit to the swamp, but his ass wouldn't answer that phone for nothing.

"Ain't nobody heard from him or Laney in a minute. Wonder what the hell they got going on. Mark said he ain't heard from none of them," Glock wondered aloud.

Ruga shrugged. "Ain't no telling. You know shit hot out there. They probably just went off the grid for a little while. Either way, we got business to handle out here. We got to focus on this shit. Can't fuck this up."

Glock hopped down off the generator that sat on the side of the abandoned building that they were using to set up shop. TJ kept his word and contacted his associate that would be joining them in a few.

"Okay, I just got off the phone with him. He's close," TJ informed as he walked back toward them.

Glock nodded his approval. "You think he going to have a problem working from this rundown ass spot? It's the closest shit I could find to the swamp."

"For the amount of money you're about to pay him, I wouldn't be surprised if he did the job on a garbage dump site," TJ joked seriously. "He's not the Hollywood type. I think you'll like him. He stands on what he believes, just like you."

Glock had his concerns and curiosities when it came to TJ's people. He was a closed-off person, so new people naturally rang bells. He didn't feed into that though. Despite how his pride made him feel, he knew it would take more than his own resources to get the job done, so he did the mature thing and went TJ's way instead of the hard way. He'd rather lose money than risk losing his homies.

Little Dave wasn't little at all, but everybody called him that because he lived in the shadow of his father, Big Dave. Big Dave was a tech wizard that used to sell high-tech devices to the government under official contract before his retirement. He was one of the main legends in the world of technology engineers. Little Dave grew up around technology and naturally became an engineer himself, but he was way more advanced than his father ever was.

"You sure that ain't Big Dave?" Ruga asked with wide eyes.

They watched as Little Dave stepped out of the RV he pulled up in. He was about 5'10" with a good amount of weight on him — too much weight, if you asked someone. He was a real fat country redneck — big blue jean shorts, brown cowboy boots, a red plaid shirt, and a grey graphic cap low on his head.

"Yup, I'm sure!" TJ chuckled. "His father is Big Dave... He may look like a supersized jellybean but don't let his dumb appearance fool you. He's twice as smart as me, and I'm probably the smartest person you know."

Glock gave TJ a grim side eye. "Just introduce us to the nigga. Let's get this show on the road."

"Alright," TJ said while shrugging smugly. "Does anybody else see a pregnant bullfrog coming this way?!" he joked loudly while looking around dramatically.

Little Dave laughed wholeheartedly. His love for TJ was shown instantly. "If I'm pregnant, it's your baby then, buddy!"

"Now, what'd I tell you about that? You don't know who the daddy is, you slut!" TJ joked as they closed the distance between them.

"I swear you're retarded," said Dave before giving TJ a big hug. "How's your mom?"

"Getting on my last nerve as usual. You know how Martha is," TJ said before turning Dave toward Glock and Ruga, who were posted up, patiently watching them. "The one with the braids is Glock, and the short one is Ruga."

Dave studied them and could instantly tell that they were some bona fide killers.

"I hear you fellas need a difficult job done," Dave stated as they neared the building.

"Exactly. Real difficult," Glock assured while looking past them at Dave's crew unloading equipment. "You trust those people with your life?"

Dave turned around to look at his crew then back at Glock with a face of confusion. "Uhmmm, yeah. Why'd you ask that?"

Ruga took a step closer to big boy, so he could hear him precisely. "Because if any one of them tells anyone about this job, people are going to die."

Dave could tell that neither Glock nor Ruga were joking one bit. "No worries. TJ gave me the rundown, and I already briefed my crew. They're solid. We've done a few joints like this for the government overseas. You're dealing with professionals. No need for the threats, buddy."

"Say no more," Glock said with a slow nod. "No more threats. Just had to make sure you're sure... Let's go inside, so I can give you another rundown."

"We'll be setting up in there as well, or is this just a meeting spot?" Dave asked while scanning the building openly.

"We're going to handle all the business here," Glock informed. "It's not the best, but this the closest spot I could secure to the swamp. The woods that surround them is what make them unreachable by the police."

Dave smiled understandably. "Oh, no worries. I've had to work in far worst conditions. As long as it has four walls that are far apart and a roof, we can work from it. Now, let me prep my team, and I'll be in there in a few," he assured before heading back toward the RV.

TJ stepped back and looked at them both. "Y'all have to chill! You can't just go around threatening everybody."

"It wasn't a threat; it was a warning, TJ. Plus, he respected it. Everything good. He alright with me so far. We about to go in here, and I'm gon' feel him out some more," Glock informed assuredly.

Thirty minutes later, while Dave's crew set up downstairs on the open floor, they strategized in an upstairs office. The place was dusty as hell but still intact. Ruga had to wipe down the table and chairs, so they'd be able to sit down.

Glock gave Dave the full rundown. Of course, he started off by letting him know exactly what type of individuals they were dealing with. "I'm not trying to capture them. I need them dead. Their past and future victims need them dead."

"I understand fully," Dave answered seriously. "This is a serious job. Taking life is no joke, but you're paying right, and most importantly, they're devils who do evil things. Makes it easier for me and my crew to sleep at night, so I'm all in."

Glock smirked. "First things first, before I pay you half of this money upfront... do you think you can really pull this shit off?"

"As long as they're not underground, I can make it happen for sure," Dave assured with confidence bigger than his belly. "Matter-a-fact, it's still light outside. We can fly over there now, run a quick recon, and we can do it tonight."

Glock shook his head in disagreement. "Nahhh, this isn't a rush job. As bad as I want it done tonight, I rather stalk my prey for a little while. That's always the best route when it comes to this type of shit."

"I like him," Dave said to TJ while pointing at Glock.

Glock reached down and grabbed the bookbag he had on the floor. "That's half. You can count it if you want," he said before sliding the bag across the table.

Dave grabbed the bag, unzipped it, and took a look inside before taking a good sniff of the money. "I'll count it later. Let's get to business. Nothing motivates me more than tax-free money."

Chapter 2

Choppa pulled up and parked his Jaguar in Careesha's driveway. He hopped out and greeted two well-known soldiers from around the way. Tory put them in charge of Careesha's security for the foreseeable future.

"What's this all about?" Choppa asked them curiously while looking back at the U-Haul truck on the curb.

"She trying to leave the city, but Tory ain't tell us nothing about that, so we called you. We supposed to be protecting her, but ain't nobody about to follow her all the way out there to the country," one of them stressed seriously.

Choppa nodded understandably. "She inside?"

They nodded in unison.

"Alright, y'all stay right here. I'll be back." Choppa walked past them into the open front door of the house.

He walked into the house and looked around. It looked good, something like he imagined it would look. "Yoo, where's Careesha?" he asked a man that was packing a pile of clothes into a suitcase.

He looked up at Choppa in a startled way but quickly shook it off once he noticed the letters BBG on Choppa's shirt. "She upstairs."

"You going to get her, or you need me to do it?" Choppa asked casually.

The man stood up to his full 5'6" length and reluctantly went upstairs to retrieve his boss. Two short minutes later, Careesha walked downstairs while taking the braids out of her head with a needle comb. "I should've known they was going to call your ass."

"What the hell is all of this?" Choppa asked curiously. "You trying to leave?"

"Nah, I'm not trying to do anything. That's what I'm about to do for sure... Unless I can't leave. Am I a hostage, Choppa?" she asked seriously with a raised brow.

That question was uncomfortable for Choppa due to the fact that she had just been held hostage by J-Rock. "Nahhh, hell nah! You not a hostage at all. You can do and go wherever you want. I'm just saying you should wait for Tory to get back. He going to be mad as fuck if he come back and you not here."

"Listen, Choppa," Careesha said seriously while taking two steps closer to him for effect, "Tory is not my man, and the last time we talked, he said I could leave if I want. Well, I made up my mind. I'm leaving. I should have listened to him at first when he told me to go back to the country."

Choppa shook his head disappointedly. He knew Careesha had potential, and Tory would feel bad about her absence upon his return. "I'm sorry for what happened to you. We was supposed to protect you," he apologized sincerely.

She flipped her hair back and took a deep breath. "It's alright, Choppa. I don't blame y'all for what happened, but it doesn't change the fact that it happened. That would've never ever happened down in the country. I'm going where I'm safe at. I took my simple life for granted. Y'all can keep all this chaos out here. I'm straight."

Choppa couldn't even respond. He just nodded his understanding before letting himself out.

"What's up?" one of his homies asked as he walked back down the driveway.

"Y'all follow her and keep watching her back until Tory gets back. Already bad enough I'm letting her leave. Can't let her leave without protection. We don't know what type of mood Tory's going to be in when he comes back."

One of them sucked his teeth and looked around unhappily. "That's that bullshit, Chop! You know it!"

"Might be, but Tory told y'all to watch her until he get back, and that's what the fuck y'all going to do. I rather play it safe," Choppa said before walking past them toward his car. "Y'all muthafuckas keep me posted," he yelled back at them. "Y'all got my number. Use it!"

Chapter 27

The sun had just disappeared from the Jamaican sky, so Isabella and Murk now had on a highly advanced set of night-vision goggles. They had viewing screens similar to Iron Man's helmet. The goggles had built-in visible GPS that highlighted the path like a bright purple rug on the ground and many other futuristic features.

"I don't think I can ever get used to these goggles," Murk admitted. "Didn't even know they made shit like these. I need to buy me a pair."

"The government has plenty of technology that's not available to the public. We had to pay ten million for six pairs of these, and that was after cashing in a favor for a discount. Shit's expensive," she informed neutrally but matter-of-factly.

They were hiking up a slight hill, using the close by trees to push themselves up. Murk studied Isabella along their journey, and two hours later, she was still moving effortlessly. Murk had good stamina, but Isabella had impeccable stamina and strength. She was the epitome of not judging a book by its cover. He would've *never* predicted that she was like this when he first laid eyes on her.

"Shitttt," Murk spat once they made it to a small clearing at the top of the hill. "These goggles say we got a hour left. You think that shit accurate?"

"If you move your ass, it will be," she teased. "You need a break, sexy?"

Murk took a series of deep breaths and shook his head. "Hell nah... Let's get this shit over with. I got this."

Isabella could hear his heavy breaths and see his chest rising. She walked over to him and placed a hand on his chest. "You're breathing too hard. You're going to have to control your breathing."

"Shit, I'm trying!" he spat irritably. "I can make it. I just need to psych myself out."

That last statement gave her an idea. She forgot about the emergency vile of cocaine she kept in her cargo pouch for emergencies. She pulled it out and dumped some on the back on her hand. "One line of this will get you rolling. Trust me. It's exactly what you need right now."

At first, Murk was about to turn her down disrespectfully, but he stopped himself. He'd never put anything up his nose before, but this was life or death, and he *needed* to keep up, so they could see the mission through.

"Fuck it!" he said before bending down and snorting the line off of her hand.

"Good shit, huh?" she asked amusingly through a beautiful smile that she loved to show. She loved her innocent appearance.

Murk nodded with wide eyes, making her laugh. "Hell yeah! *Shitttt!*"

"Shhhhhh!" she spat sternly with a stiff index finger to his lip. "They might have scouts out here. Come on, let's go. We have a tight window to execute."

****

A little under an hour later, Isabella and Murk had made it safely to J-Rock's compound. That was the easy part. The hard part was coming next.

"Okay then," Isabella said before doing a line of coke for herself. "This is where shit is about to get real. The key to an attack like this is to work smart and not hard."

116

Murk nodded understandably. The coke did him some major justice for the circumstance. His breathing was under control, and he wasn't even nervous about the mission anymore. He was locked in. He was all in. "What you need me to do?"

"I need you to stay right here while I go do the job," she informed simply after handing him the bookbag off her back.

Murk's face crumbled. "You got me bent. I got to come with you to watch your back."

"If you come with me, you're going to slow me down, and we're going to get caught, then I'm going to end up using you as a shield. That's something I don't want to happen because I actually like you, so stay right here and be ready for the trip back because it's going to be at a much quicker pace," she instructed carefully before bolting across the clear landing with nothing but the sword on her back.

"I think I'm in love with that bitch," Murk told himself audibly as she made her way onto the compound.

It was clear that J-Rock didn't expect anyone to attack him on his hidden compound. Most people didn't know about it, and most people wouldn't have the balls, but the Gulf Port Cartel was known for doing deeds that most were afraid to do, and Isabella was their secret weapon — a one-woman army at its finest.

The compound consisted of a handful of warehouse-like buildings that were scattered amongst the trees. The trees on the compound weren't as thick as the rest of the forest, but they were still there, and that was all Isabella needed.

She had a pistol holstered on her hip for an emergency, but the chances of her using it was very slim. She was the Grim Reaper with her sword and should be able to complete the mission with it.

After clearing the grass clearing, she hid behind a tree to check the coast. Once she saw that everything was clear, she headed to the first building. The four men sharing beer over a game of soccer didn't see or hear her. She was like a breeze of fresh air as she bolted past them less that fifteen feet away.

She hid by another tree once she saw another dreaded man with a beer head out of the first building. He took a casual scroll around the building, walking toward the rest of the buildings behind it. She pushed off of the tree and darted toward the man with cheetah-like speed.

"Don't move and don't yell," she whispered in his ear from behind.

She had the blade of her sword pressed hard on his throat, causing him to drop his bottle of beer on the ground. Luckily for her, there was grass on the ground, so the bottle thumped on the ground instead of shattering.

"Me don't know who you is, but you bark up the wrong tree, Miss," he warned in a thick, Jamaican accent.

"I'm going to cut your head off and nail it to a tree if you don't tell me where J-Rock is," she threatened seriously.

"He's... in that building right there," he answered a little too quickly for her.

She knew he was lying, so she slit his neck with precision. He tried to yell and alert his comrades, but nothing but blood came out of his mouth. He gripped his neck with both hands as he dropped down to his knees. She kicked him in the back, causing him to fall forward onto the ground, and hopped right over him as she continued past the first building.

"You think he was lying?" Murk asked from the small communication device in her ear.

"I know he lied. That's why I killed him," she answered casually. "If you see those other guys make their way around this side of the building, I want you to put that rifle to work. Light their asses up, and I'll be on my way to you. We'll have to make a run for it. We're on a even tighter timeframe now, so be ready because either way, we're about to be hauling ass back through that forest... No breaks this time so collect your breath now."

"I'm good… Just be safe, man," Murk stressed seriously, not hiding the concern in his tone.

"Aww, you're too cute," she whispered as she made her way to the second building where the dead man said J-Rock was.

She knew J-Rock wasn't in that building, so that meant he had to be in one of the other two. She took a deep breath and darted past the first building with her sword in hand. She ran into two men who were walking by on patrol.

"Aye, you…" One of them tried to say something, but she sliced his throat open with a quick strike of her blade.

The other man tried to raise his rifle, but she spun around while taking a step closer to him. By the time she was finished spinning, the other man was looking at her through wide eyes of disbelief. He couldn't believe how fast she moved. He dropped his rifle and grabbed his neck once he noticed she had managed to strike him with her blade.

Isabella stood there emotionlessly while watching the life slip out of him. "I can tell you're the type that's used to ending up on top of situations like this judging by the look of disbelief in your eyes. It's okay though. Can't win every battle. You're quick with that gun, Rasta man, but unfortunately for you, I'm way quicker with this sword," she taunted before darting off toward the buildings.

Chapter 28

J-Rock was in his personal quarters with Vanya, relieving some stress on her little ass. He had her pinned down on the soft rug on the floor as he dropped every inch of his dick into her.

"Baby, you're fucking the Mario coins out of a bitch tonight! Pull my hair and slap this ass!" she commanded challengingly. She'd become a lot more aggressive than she was when they first started fucking with each other. He had surely turned her into a savage.

"Bitch, you think you ready for this shit, huh?" he asked excitedly. The devilish sneer on his face was one of pure excitement. She didn't have to tell him twice.

He grabbed a handful of her silky hair and yanked her head back toward him. "I'm gon' make you fall in love with this dick all over again!"

"Yesssss, Daddy! Make me fall in love with that big ass dick! Fuck it! Shove it in my ass!" she requested frantically. She'd always loved sex, but he had turned her into a whole nymphomaniac.

J-Rock chuckled as he snatched his dick out of her soaking wetness and navigated himself into her asshole. He used her pussy juices as lubricant to help him bust into her tight hole.

"I love that dick, man!" she exclaimed so seriously while looking back at him.

She wanted to see his face, but she was met with a scary surprise. Her eyes grew wide when she laid eyes on the woman that stood behind her man with a sword cocked all the way back. Before she could even muster a syllable, J-Rock's head was separated from his body, making its way down to the floor.

Blood squirted out from his neck, where his head used to be, as his body collapsed onto the floor on top of his head. His reign of terror was brought to an end just like that.

"Oh, my God!" Vanya said in disbelief as she wiped some of his blood off of her face.

Isabella snatched the sheet off of the bed and bent down to wrap J-Rock's head in it. Vanya's training kicked in, and she took the opportunity to pounce on her husband's killer. She was livid with anger.

"Move another inch and you're going to join him," Isabella promised after standing back up quickly. She heard Vanya trying to get up off the floor to sneak her. "I don't like killing women, but I definitely will tonight though. Don't test me, honey."

The next thing she knew, she heard gunshots erupt. "Get up out of there, Issy!" Murk spat urgently, calling her by the nickname he'd given her.

"Aghhhh!" Vanya yelled as she jumped onto Isabella. She had managed to get to her feet while Isabella was distracted by the gunshots, so she seized the opportunity.

She jumped on Isabella and tried to tackle her to the ground, but Isabella deflected the tackle, and Vanya ended up falling to the floor by herself.

"You want to be with your man, huh?" Isabella asked irritably while standing over Vanya with a grimace.

"Fuck you, bitch!" Vanya spat fearlessly while looking up at Isabella with a sneer. "I'll never be a victim again. I'll die with my head up before..."

Isabella cut her sentence short by plunging her sword into Vanya's face. The blade came through the other side. She didn't even bother to take it out. She just let Vanya keep it as a parting gift. "All you had to do was listen, girl. You could've found you another man, silly."

She shook her head at Vanya one last time and quickly bent back down to collect J-Rock's head. After she had his head wrapped securely in the sheet, she darted out of the building to go help Murk.

"Where are you?" she asked Murk from the earpiece.

"Same spot!" he spat. "You don't see them niggas that got me pinned down?" he asked before letting off a few shots in their direction to keep them off of his tail.

"It's the four guys that were playing soccer. J-Rock didn't have as much protection as we thought. His ass felt safe out here," Isabella concluded. "Stay where you are."

Isabella pulled out her pistol and started letting loose on them, diverting their attention. "Chop them down now!" she commanded after taking cover behind a thick tree.

"Say no more!" Murk spat before popping up and carefully picking off two of the four Jamaicans.

Isabella popped out from behind the tree and shot the last two guys in the back as they tried to flee for cover. "I thought he was going to have way more security than that. His ass obviously felt safe out here. Didn't think anybody would come touch his ass out here."

"So, that means we don't got to haul ass through these woods, right?" he asked once she was in speaking distance because he had turned his earpiece off.

She nodded. "Correct, but we still have to keep a steady pace because we have to beat the sun. If we don't catch that flight, we'll be stuck out here for a week, and I'm not going to let that happen," she said after turning her own earpiece off.

"That's cool and all, but I'm going to need to see the head for myself before we go anywhere," he insisted seriously.

She started to decline his request until she looked him in the eyes and saw the direness. There was no telling how much trauma J-Rock had caused him, and it was obviously personal, so she handed him the head.

Murk accepted the head from her and placed it on the ground carefully before unwrapping it. He sighed a deep sigh of relief when he saw J-Rock's face. He looked surprised as he looked up at Murk.

"I'll see you in hell, nigga. Hope you understand though. You had to go, bruh. You was poisonous to the empire. I'll keep shit in line for you though and make sure your name is remembered in them streets," he promised before wrapping his head back up with care. "Alright, let's go, baby girl."

Chapter 29

"Listen here, nephew, I know you was out there doing your thing. I've been hearing these boys in here talk about you, some out of respect but most out of fear. It's clear you been doing the devil's work out there, but now is the time to reflect and rebuild," the old head told Swiss as he leaned on the concrete wall with his arms folded.

He was one of those old niggas who'd been in and out of prison his whole life. He had a body full of prison tattoos and muscles from head to toe.

"What you in here for? God's work?" Swiss asked, heavy on the sarcasm. He was lying down on his back on his bunk, staring at the top bunk.

At the commissioner's request, the hospital released Swiss early into police custody. They wanted to go ahead and get the wheel rolling on his official arrest. They made a big deal of it. There were a half dozen news cameras and two dozen reporters trying to get a statement out of Swiss as he was being escorted out of the hospital. The mayor and the police commissioner held a whole press conference about the notorious menace they'd finally taken off the streets, totally disregarding the fact that he saved those people at the lounge. They needed a villain to make an example out of, and Swiss was unfortunately that person.

"Actually, I am. Some dumb ass broke into my home while my wife and kids was there. I killed him with my bare hands," the old head informed seriously with intense eyes.

Swiss nodded. "I give you that. You were justified with that. You not even supposed to be in here right now then."

"The judge didn't care nothing about me acting out of defense for the safety of my family. All he heard was a repeated offender killed someone, so here I am, about to spend the rest of my years in prison." There was no anger in his voice, just raw acceptance.

The old steel doors opened loudly, and Swiss sat up as fast as he could. His midsection was still in pain from the surgery, even though he was making a speedy recovery. He needed at least two more weeks in the hospital, but the law wanted to play it dirty. They put him in solitary confinement for forty-eight hours before sticking him in general population that morning.

The whole jailhouse was talking about him. It was rare that a Vulture was handcuffed. The three Vultures that the police ran down on in the past went down in blazes of glory. Swiss was the first Vulture that they'd apprehended on a major offense.

"Uhmmm, you might want to tighten up, young buck. It's eight BBG boys on the way up here right now!" the old head warned urgently.

"Aaagghhh!" Swiss grimaced as he stood up as fast as he could.

He was in pain, but he fought through it like the warrior he was. He gritted his teeth as he looked around the room for a quick weapon. "Pass me that broom in the corner," he told the old head while pointing at the wooden broom.

The old head quickly tossed Swiss the broom and hurried back to the front of the cell to meet the mob of goons. "Woahhh now! It's eight of you niggas and one of him. He's not even to full health. The man's still healing from surgery. You don't get points from that."

"That bitch ass nigga killed my cousin!" one of them spat angrily. "Get the fuck out of the way or you gone be on our list too, OG. Think about your family out there!" They knew the old head was nice with his hands and would easily take half of them out, so they had to threaten his family.

"It's aight, OG! Get out the way!" Swiss commanded firmly.

He clutched the broom tightly and prepared himself to fight for his life. He refused to beg for mercy. If he had to die, it would be on his feet like the gangsta he was. "Bring y'all bitch ass on! Let's get it!" he barked painfully.

The old head stepped aside, and the BBG members flooded into the cell. Swiss caught the first nigga with a broom to the head, sending him backward, but the rest bum-rushed him. He managed to clock another nigga in the head before he was tackled to the ground.

"Aghhhhhh!" he roared before sinking his teeth into the nigga's face that had tackled him. He locked in on the nigga like a lion and literally bit off a chunk of his cheek.

The others began to stomp Swiss out on the ground as their comrade screamed like a little bitch while rolling around on the ground, holding his face.

"Fuck it!" the old head spat before springing into action.

He couldn't take it anymore. He respected Swiss for holding his own against impossible odds, but he couldn't just sit there and watch them kill the young nigga. He saw so much potential in Swiss, and God wouldn't let him stand by and watch him die, so he took action.

The BBG members — and everybody else in the jailhouse — knew about Old School's fighting abilities. He had to make a few light examples not too long ago, but they'd never seen him in full throttle mode. Old School started swinging, and niggas started dropping like limp noodles. He knocked out three niggas before the jail guards made it to the cell and filled the room with thick pepper spray.

The strong assaulting stench of the spray in the small, stuffy room took the fight out of everyone as they got on the ground like the guards ordered. Old School ended up on the ground next to Swiss. "You still alive, youngblood?" he asked Swiss with one blurry eye open. The other one burned too much to open.

"Yeah, nigga! Thanks to you," Swiss admitted with both his eyes closed. It was his first time being maced, and the shit was killing him. "I'm gon' make sure your family good though!" he promised with both eyes squeezed shut. He couldn't see Old School, but he knew he was close.

"Just focus on your breathing, youngin," Old School coached. He was a veteran convict and had been hit with pepper spray more than a few times, so he was more immune to it than the others.

Swiss listened to Old School and focused on breathing. He kept thinking about how shit would've turned out if Old School hadn't jumped in because he intervened right before they were about to start stabbing him up. They would've surely killed him before the guards could respond. Then, he went to wondering if it was God that drove Old School to jump in and save him.

Chapter 30

The day had finally come that Glock had been deeply anticipating. He paced the ground in front of the six monster drones that were lined up in front of them. He stood there with Dave and his crew as they prepared for takeoff. Glock felt weird about the whole situation to be honest. He was used to being hands on and taking out his target the old-fashioned way. This was something totally foreign.

"You did final checks on all of the birds?" Dave asked his head mechanic technician.

He gave Dave the thumbs up, and Dave held his phone up to his ear. "Let em rip!" he ordered before taking several steps back.

Everybody else did the same. The pilots were in their own tent inside the building. Their job was the most important, so they flew in isolation to minimize distractions and mistakes.

"Damn, them bitches loud!" Glock spat while covering his ears. All six drone blades were louder than a helicopter.

"Told you to put on the headphones!" Dave teased as they watched the birds lift into the evening sky.

Glock took his fingers out of his ears when the birds got high into the sky. A few seconds later, they disappeared into the clouds.

"What now?" Glock asked awkwardly.

Dave pointed back firmly at the building. "We head back inside to the operation room. This is where all the magic happens," he explained excitedly after taking his headphones off.

Dave and Glock headed to the operation room where a few analysts were already stationed. They were watching live footage from the multiple cameras that were on each drone. It was a big tent with dozens of monitor screens.

"Damn!" Glock said, openmouthed. The lenses on the drones were immaculate. He felt like he was flying in the sky himself while looking at the screens.

"Here you go," Dave said, passing him an operation headset, so he could be in the full loop.

Glock was there to oversee the mission with Dave. He wanted Ruga to share this moment with him, but Dave was insistent on having his workspace as less crowded as possible. Glock wanted him to get the job done correctly, so he respected Dave's workspace. He wanted them to be as comfortable as possible.

The drones only took ten short minutes to reach the swamp. "Alright! Form a perimeter around the premises and park the birds high up until the sun retires for the night," he ordered the pilots. "Standby for orders.

"Alright, put those cameras to work. I need visuals. Find me some targets!" he commanded the analysts in the room. They got to work and started using the zoom on the mini satellite cameras.

"I ain't gon' lie. This some real *Mission Impossible* ass shit," Glock admitted, not even trying to hide his excitement. He felt like a kid in a toy store. "So, you telling me those drones are about to go hunt those folks down and take them out? Just like that?"

Dave looked at him with a big, child-like grin. "Yuuuuup! Those are elite death machines you just watched take off into the sky. Capable of taking out half of a football stadium if put in the wrong hands."

"Damnnn, boy... I gots to see this shit for myself," Glock stated before spotting movement on one of the monitors.

"*Bingo!* We got action!" he spat with wide eyes while pointing at one of the large HD monitors.

"Good eyes, brodie!" Dave applauded Glock with a pat on the shoulder. "Lock in on that boat!" he ordered the analyst who controlled the camera on the drone nearest to the boat.

They zoomed in on the small speed boat and started snapping pictures of the two hairy Caucasian men aboard. Dave blew their faces up on one of the screens. "Recognize these two?" he asked after turning his head to Glock.

"Yeah, that one with the longest beard is one of the ones the sheriff said he wants alive," Glock said while pulling up the pictures of the three men that the sheriff wanted alive on his phone.

"Don't lose that boat!" Dave spat before walking up closer to the monitor.

Glock followed. "You think they got another lil' spot out there?"

"I'll bet my mama's left titty they do," Dave answered seriously. "From the sound of it, these folks are too organized not to. The sheriff is smart for wanting to capture a few of them."

A few minutes later, the boat led them to another hidden village on the swamp. "*Bingo!*" Dave shouted out with a fist pump.

"What now?" Glock asked. He wanted to see the drones in action, but he didn't want to seem like a bloodthirsty maniac, so he played it cool.

"It's time to get *down and dirty,*" Dave informed sinisterly with a wink.

Dave got on his radio and ordered the pilots to split up. Three drones flew over to the original stronghold, and the other three stationed at the hidden swamp village that their targets had just led them to.

They did another twenty minutes of reckon until the sun was well-rested. The drones had immaculate military grade night vision lenses and a lot of other features. "Damn, so we can see them moving inside the huts too?" Glock asked with wide eyes.

Dave nodded proudly. "Yuuuup! Along with the night vision, we have heat sensors. Anything with a strong heartbeat shows up red. See, look. You can even see the gators in the water."

"That's harddd," Glock complimented. "So, when do we get this shit crackin'?"

"Now!" Dave informed before barking back-to-back orders.

The drones swooped down on both villages at the same time and went to work. Glock just stood there, openmouthed and wide-eyed. He couldn't believe how lethal and efficient the drones were. They took out targets with bullets that went through the wooden cabins and shot the sheriff's targets with high-dosage tranquilizers. Both attacks were over with in less than two minutes.

"Nine targets dead on both sites and two tranquilized. Tell the sheriff we couldn't identity the last one on his list. He also needs to get a chopper out there to rescue those children and women."

Glock looked at the five kids and three women on the monitor. He couldn't see them clearly because they were inside one of the huts, but he saw their body figures through the heat sensors. They were all piled up and balled up in the corner of one of the huts. They were as still as statues, obviously scared to move a muscle after all the gunfire.

"Those are the hostages that we saved, huh?" Dave asked with heavy satisfaction. He was thankful that he was able to use his abilities for good.

"Yeah, man," Glock answered with satisfaction of his own. "They safe now because of us, bruh."

Dave put a heavy hand on Glock's shoulders. "Go ahead and call the sheriff, so they can rescue those victims and clean up that mess. Our job is done."

Chapter 31

The next day, Isabella and Murk found their way back to Columbia safely with J-Rock's head in a mini cooler.

"I never been so happy to see this nigga alive," Tory joked seriously, referring to Murk, as they watched them make their way up the driveway.

Diablo laughed. "You're funny, bro!"

Diablo ended up checking in on Tory more, and Tory ended up dropping his guard toward him. They'd done a lot of coke and shared a lot of stories in the last three days. They'd both grown on each other.

"Hold on, man. I got to see this shit for myself," Tory spat before stepping forward to meet them. "That's him?" he asked Murk. "Open that bitch up. I got to see right now."

Isabella started to say no, but Murk stopped her and sat the cooler down for Tory. Although he didn't like Tory, he understood the need for him to see J-Rock's head for himself. He had also been tormented by J-Rock for years. It was about the *only* thing they had in common.

Tory opened the cooler slowly, and J-Rock's eyes looked up at him. The back of his head was buried in the ice. "I don't know how they did it, but they got yo' bitch ass," he said before snapping a quick picture with his phone. Diablo had awarded them their phones back that morning.

"Alright, let's get this ceremony out the way, so you guys can catch your flight," Diablo said before walking into the house.

Murk closed the cooler and continued into the house. "Miss me?" he asked Laney as he passed her.

"Actually, I did, nigga. I been praying for your yellow ass," she answered truthfully.

He smiled. "I appreciate that, baby girl," he said gratefully before following the train of people into the house.

****

Everybody wasn't allowed at the ceremony — just Laney, Tory, and Murk. They were brought straight to the worship room. It was a big room with no windows that was painted black with symbols drawn all over the walls with red paint. Over fifty candles burned from the floor to the ceiling. They were all sitting down on the floor inside of two triangles that were drawn on top of each other on the floor.

"Don't make a move or a sound. Remain completely still and quiet during this ritual," Diablo instructed as he walked into the room butt ass naked. His entire body was covered in human blood.

All three of them looked at him through wide eyes of shock, but no one dared to make a move or a sound. They just sat there and let Diablo do his thing. It wasn't like they could reject it. It was something that they had to see through, the price they had to pay for the money they made off of the cartel.

Diablo had J-Rock's head in his right arm, like a football. He sat it down in between them and backed up to the podium. "These are the newest subjects to our dynasty!" he said before saying something else in Spanish.

"Stand up!" he ordered sharply.

They stood.

"Now lay down, face first, with your bodies straight as a pencil!"

They looked at each other then back at him.

"*Lay downnnn!*" he commanded forcefully with a little extra force behind him. It was like a demon was yelling the shit with him like in the movies.

They quickly laid on the ground with their faces buried into the floor.

"Now, repeat after me!" he instructed in his regular voice.

"I give my soul to Satan and his mother! I give my soul to the cartel! Take my soul. It is yours to keep! Take my body! From my head to my feet!"

He made them repeat that chant eighteen times before blowing foul smelling smoke in each of their faces individually. After that, he pissed on his own hands and rubbed it into their hair. Once he was done violating them, he left the room without another word.

"You're free to pack your belongings and leave. You're done here," one of his advisors informed after sticking his head in the door.

"Bruhhhh, what the fuck was that all about?" Tory asked with a crumbled face.

Murk shrugged nonchalantly. "At this point in our life, after all the shit we done been through, it shouldn't even faze us. Just put this shit behind you and try not to think about it. At least we survived this trip."

"Facts! Now, let's get up out this creepy ass room. My skin crawling," said Laney. "Nasty ass nigga done rubbed piss on us! Come on y'all. I'll be damned if we miss that damn flight... And not another word about this shit to *anybody*. We take this shit to the grave," she spat.

Murk and Turk gave her looks that could kill. That last sentence didn't even have to be spoken out loud.

They packed and showered as fast as they could before heading to the airport. Tory said his goodbyes to Diablo's crazy ass, and Murk said his goodbyes to Isabella's crazy ass. Karmen and Laney didn't say goodbye to anyone. They were in the limo before anybody else. They were ready to get back to the States and hopefully never have to return to that godforsaken place.

"Laney," Karmen called as Laney was looking out the window at them saying their goodbyes.

Laney turned to her. "Yes?"

"I'm sorry you had to go through that," she apologized sincerely. "I tried to shield you from all this, but it obviously didn't work out like that. It's out the way now, and you're untouchable. I won't let anything, or anyone, touch you!"

"It's okay, Mommy," Laney assured gently. "I understand that it comes with a price. I'm just glad a bitch survived it all... I'm just ready to get home to Mini now."

Karmen's face lit up. "Awwwww, yeah! I can't wait to meet my granddaughter face-to-face for the first time."

Chapter 32

Almost three weeks had passed since Laney had been back from Columbia, and shit was smoother than a balloon covered in melted butter. There was peace in the city, and Rock Nation was running smoothly. J-Rock had turned into a myth, and they kept his name alive in the streets. Only a handful of people knew J-Rock was dead, and that was how it was going to stay.

It was safe to say that she was officially out of the game. She let Murk and Tory take over as a unit, and she was able to step all the way into the corporate world like she wanted.

On top of the gigantic investment Static had acquired for her, she had other investments she'd been looking at over the months. Now, she had the time and energy to weed through them and pursue the ones that fit her best. She had to have a series of meetings with her new legal team first though.

She sat back and watched as Karmen taught Mini how to swim in their backyard pool because the inside pool was being cleaned. She wanted to go live and share the experience with her followers, but Karmen quickly shut that down. She carefully let Mini know that she was not to be filmed or posted. Of course, Mini had questions, but like she did with Laney, she minded her business.

"It's *soooo* good to have my queen back in her kingdom by my side," Zion confessed as he walked up to her.

He had just walked out of the back door of the house with his gym clothes on. He had just left the gym, but he was back early.

"It's good to be back, and I'll never leave again... Why you back so early? Everything okay?"

"Shittt, I missed y'all, so I cut the day short," he informed nonchalantly. "The fight is in two months. I'm ready for that nigga, so I don't have to train as hard."

Laney looked up at her man seriously and tapped the reclined chair next to her. Zion took a seat and placed a gentle hand on her bare thigh. "What's up?" he asked.

"I'm here one hundred percent now, and I can be in your corner how I need to be. For the past few days, I've been studying your opponent. He's not to be underestimated. I know you're good... No, you're great at what you do, but I'm going to need you to fight this man like your life depends on it. I can't lose you. He gave a man mild brain damage in that ring before, baby. Don't sleep on him."

Zion nodded understandably. "I'm not underestimating him, baby. I'm just saying that I'm ready. I'm ready-ready. I can afford to take a half day and spend the rest of it with my beloved family."

"Awwww, you so sweet!" she said with a poked-out lip. "I could've sworn you was going to start switching on a bitch when you got out, but to my surprise, you're keeping it solid, baby. I thank you *soooo* much for that because I know I'm not easy to deal with every day."

Zion chuckled. "Well, now you see this shit for yourself. I love the fuck out of you, woman, and I'll go to the end of the earth about you. I care about you way more than you know. I can focus and breathe easy now though since you out them streets. Lord knows I was praying like a muthafucka for you."

"I'm free now, baby," she assured seriously after sitting up in the chair, facing him. "Now, I can be the wife you deserve. Plus, I need to be there every second of this baby boy's life," she joked while rubbing her growing stomach.

"Baby boy?" He looked at her sideways. "We never talked about that there. What if I wanted a girl?"

"Oh, noooo! This better be a damn boy!"

Zion's face crumbled a little. "So, if we have a girl, you going to be mad?"

"Yuuuup!" she spat with a neck roll.

"That's fucked up, bruh," he said disappointedly after taking his hand off her thigh.

"Aww, I'm just playing, Daddy!" she assured sincerely as she got up to go sit in his lap. "You know I'm going to love that child to death regardless, but I do prefer a little baby boy."

"That's cool because I don't got a problem with a boy. He gone be so nice with the hands. Them kids gone know early not to fuck with him," he boasted like the proud father he was soon to be.

Laney just leaned in and rested her face on the top of his head. They hugged each other and just took in the moment.

"Zion! You getting in the water? Mommy pulling the pregnant card, so I couldn't argue with that!" Mini yelled from the other side of the pool.

"Here I come, baby!" he informed before leaning in to give Laney a kiss. "I love you, beautiful muthafucka."

"I love you too, Zaddy," she said before sitting back in her original chair and watching Zion do a cannonball into the pool and swim toward Mini and Karmen.

Laney took a deep breath and reached for her tray of sliced pickles and grapes. Life was good on her end.

Chapter 33

Meanwhile, in Durham, there was a big outside event taking place on the church's massive lawn. It was a county festival that Glock sponsored and planned with Pastor Mack. There were tons of festivities there and hundreds of people. People from both sides of Durham County came together in celebration of God's work. Eight kids and women were returned safely to their loved ones from both ends of the county lines. It was a celebration of life, and it brought the town together for the first time in a long time.

The sheriff pulled some strings together to get a chopper and save the hostages. The Sheriff's Department took credit for bringing down the untouchable crew of rapists, killers, and cannibals. The big bosses in the department didn't ask too many questions since there were no casualties besides the predators. It was a big win for the department and the type of case they'd been needing too.

That was the story for outsiders, but all the locals knew the real story. Glock and his wolves got the job done — a job that most were too scared — or failed — to do. They didn't know that Glock outsourced to get it done, and he didn't plan on telling anyone. All that mattered was that he was capable of getting a muthafucka touched, even in a difficult place. He was a force to be reckoned with, and that was the image he needed portrayed around those parts.

Pastor Mack linked up with Pastor Manning to host the event, just to show the town that they were leading by example. They both had different points of views on life, but they both wanted the best for the town, so they built on that. They were on a stage, performing a quick joint sermon for the crowd. There was both a Black and white audience in attendance. Both pastors spoke their peace and announced their plans on bringing the town together.

Everyone knew the lines would still be there at the end of the day. They were too different to coexist in an everyday sense, but the respect and peace was what the pastors sought. Glock was a part of the audience, and he listened carefully because he actually respected what they were saying and what they were trying to do. Pastor Manning might've been a little uptight like Pastor Mack said, but he didn't share the Aryans' point-of-view, so he was alright with Glock.

"Aye, y'all! Watch out! Here come these niggas!" one of Glock's youngins announced as he ran toward them. Ruga had him on lookout.

Glock turned around and spotted the line of pickup trucks pulling into the parking lot. "Come on, y'all!" Glock ordered before leading the way down the field. He was trying to get out of the festival area, where the civilians were, just in case things got heated.

Polar Bear hopped out of his truck and led the gang of Aryans to approach Glock.

"Not today!" Glock shouted twenty feet out. "Your day will come, but today isn't about me or you. It's about the town. Let them have this day."

Polar Bear continued walking and closing the distance. He was a big and powerful man, but he was soft spoken and didn't want to strain his voice. He stopped eight feet away. "I didn't come here for all that, man. Calm down."

"So, what's up?" Glock asked with a raised brow. "Ain't nothing to talk about. May the last king stand. The sheriff gone let us do our shit as long as it ain't no civilian casualties. I just bought a whole trailer park for y'all asses. We about to turn that bitch into a *Call of Duty* warzone, just to make sure no innocents catch a stray. We gangsta for real. We gon' fight tooth and nail until the very end. You gon' have to kill us all because we don't fold against the odds."

Polar Bear just stood there with a face of pure astonishment. He had never witnessed anyone so passionate about battle. Glock was a true warrior, and he respected that. He would always have hate for the Black race, but that didn't mean he was stupid. Glock was obviously not the problem he needed in his life at the moment, so he made a leader's decision. "Listen, I've collected enough from Pastor Mack over the years, and I've decided to leave it at that. I'm going to leave this side of Durham to you as long as you don't step on my toes. We could just stay out of each other's way and keep the peace out here. I respect what the pastors are trying to do out here. You get me?"

His statement threw Glock for a loop. He wasn't expecting that response at all. It took him a second to respond. "Shittt, I guess I'm cool with that. Save losses on both ends."

"So, we're good?" Polar Bear asked before reaching his hand out for a shake.

Glock looked down at Polar Bear's hand, back at his guys, to the growing crowd of civilians behind them, and back to Polar Bear. "Yeah, we good, bruh... As long as the respect is there. I'm super big on that," he warned carefully before shaking the enemy's hand.

"And that right there, ladies and gentlemen, is what a united Durham looks like!" Pastor Mack shouted, causing the crowd to start clapping, applauding their growth.

Pastor Manning tried to get the Aryans to stay and enjoy the festival, but they had business to handle. Everybody else went back to the festivities, and Glock made his way over to the food tent. His gang was really hungry, but it was still an excuse to see his new favorite person.

"I'm proud of you, handsome," Kelsey said as a greeting when he walked up to her.

"That means a lot, baby girl," he responded while leaning on the counter stylishly. "You going to work the whole time? I'm trying to show you a good time. Win you a stuffed animal or some shit."

Kelsey giggled sweetly while covering her face to cover the brief blush. She knew Glock wasn't used to being gentle with women, but his efforts were cute as ever.

"I'll take a break in thirty minutes."

"That's perfect!" he informed with satisfaction. "We should be done eating by then."

"What you want, boy? The menu isn't the biggest, but the food's good," she informed truthfully.

Glock and his gang ordered their food and waited impatiently for the cook to prepare their orders.

Chapter 34

Tory was back in business, and the dollars were rolling in like never before. With J-Rock out of the picture, they didn't have to pay him a large cut, so Rock Nation's entire fortune was split three ways. He split profits evenly with Laney and Murk monthly. Before, they only received a fraction of their current pay. J-Rock used to get sixty-five percent of everything. So, they were seeing way more money these days as the heads of the organization.

Tory didn't think it was fair since neither of them would be taking risks anymore, but he didn't have a say-so. Plus, it wasn't his fault that they were distancing themselves from the street life, building legit fronts to wash their money, and he didn't. It was all good though because, little did they know, Tory had big plans of his own.

He paid several suburban men and women from around his way to fly out to Vegas and place multiple bets for hundreds of thousands of dollars apiece. He decided to go along with Big Body's wishes and went all in on Zion's fight. The betting odds were stacked high against Zion, so the four million that Tory had placed on the fight would turn into just over thirty million if Zion came out on top.

After paying the carriers their hush money, he would still come out with over twenty-seven million dollars in legit money. Then, he planned on funding BBG Records and give some of his soldiers a shot. It was a win-win, but Zion had to win first. He had faith in the nigga though.

"We almost there," Choppa informed, breaking Tory's train of thought.

They sat in the back of a 2016 Escalade truck that was in the middle of a presidential motorcade. There were twenty vehicles driving in front of the Escalade and twenty vehicles driving behind it. A few local sheriff cruisers voluntarily followed the motorcade because that wasn't the type of thing you saw every day in the little town of Lillington where the population was barely over six thousand.

Most people around that way had never seen that many vehicles move as one, so when all of those vehicles flooded into Campbell Creek Apartments, nobody knew what to expect. It was the only low-income apartment complex in town, so it was big as hell. The vehicles drove to the heart of the complex and crowded the street where Careesha's building sat.

Over a hundred BBG members piled out of the vehicles. There were some men with automatic rifles, some beautiful women with dresses and heels, and even some children. Tenants began to come out of their apartments out of curiosity once more police cruisers pulled up. The whole sheriff's department was out there supervising the historic visit.

Tory finally hopped out of the truck and walked up to Choppa and a few other team leaders who were speaking in a huddle.

"What y'all niggas over here talking about?" Tory asked while fixing his Gucci t-shirt and adjusting his Tampa Bay baseball cap. "Y'all niggas got a problem with my lil' pit stop?" he asked half-jokingly.

"Hell nah, nigga!" Choppa instantly assured. "I would've did the same about my bitch... We over here brainstorming on ways to improve the business and minimize the risk."

Tory nodded. "Y'all niggas always on the job. I like that."

"That's our job, so you won't have so much on your plate, big dawg," one of the lieutenants added seriously. "This a whole different level of money, and we just want to make sure we do right with the shit." His name was Money, and he was currently the biggest hustler in BBG.

Tory was about to ask them about their ideas when a handful of soldiers approached them. "The police telling us we got to go."

"Oh, shit!" Choppa spat while looking past them. "They got this nigga, Nitro, talking to the damn sheriff!"

Tory took off jogging before he could even finish, and the rest of them followed. Everybody moved to Tory's beat, and it showed. That didn't go unnoticed by the sheriff either. "Just chill, Nitro. I got this," Tory said while putting an arm on his shoulder.

Nitro instantly calmed down and let the air out of his chest — as if the officers were saved by Tory. "Tell them we gon' leave when we ready."

"I'm afraid my comrade is correct on his statement though," Tory said, addressing the authorities. "We're not causing anyone harm, but I have unfinished business in these apartments, and I'm not leaving without it... Y'all are welcome to spectate because this is your jurisdiction, but remember, y'all don't have jurisdiction over us. We'll be out of y'all lil' town soon enough," he stated matter-of-factly before walking off back toward Careesha's building.

****

Careesha was awakened by her best friend, Kadesha. "Girllll! Get the fuck up! It's a thousand people out there for you! They keep asking for you. Police out there and all! I'm scared, girl! What the hell is going on?" she informed frantically.

"What?!" Careesha spat as she popped out of her sleep like someone had thrown a bucket of ice-cold water on her. "Let me see!"

Careesha jumped up and ran past her friend, out the room, so she could look out the living room window at the front. Her eyes grew wide when she saw the whole scene. "This nigga done lost his fucking mind!"

"What?"

"Stay here, girl," she instructed before throwing her hair braids in a ponytail, sliding on some slippers, and racing out of the house. The spandex biker shorts and halter top would have to do.

"Where's Tory?" she asked once she was downstairs.

The group of boys she asked were smiling at her as they all pointed in Tory's direction. All eyes were on her as she made her way to Tory. He was leaning comfortably on the hood of his truck, engaged in a conversation about sports, when she walked up. "Tory, what the hell is all this?"

"You see how I'm coming about you, baby!" he said with his hands outstretched.

She gave him a wide-eyed look of disbelief. "First, you had them two niggas following a bitch all around the state, now this?"

"Yup!" Tory answered unapologetically. "I told you I won't never let *nothing* happen to you again. Why the hell you move back out here? You bigger than this, shawty. Your place is by my side in that queen's throne. You selling yourself short out here, baby girl. Not even gonna lie."

"Mannnn... You got too much going on out there," she stated as gruesome flashbacks attacked her mind. She grimaced a little.

Tory pushed off of the truck and closed the distance between them. "J-Rock's dead, girl... Told you I would handle it. Nigga head got cut off and all," he whispered in her ear before backing up some to see her expression.

She just stood there, openmouthed, lost for words. She didn't even know how to feel about that yet.

"But yeah though. I'm here for what's mines and not leaving without it," he informed seriously. "All you got to do is go get dressed and bring your ass. I'll buy you a whole new wardrobe on the road. BBG about to go on tour, just to show our faces and campaign for the brand."

"It's going to take me a little while to get ready, boy. I just woke up," she informed with a smile.

Tory shrugged. "We got time. You can bring your lil' friend if you want to. I'll buy her a wardrobe too. Or put her on Choppa so he can pay for it." He looked at her sidekick standing in the distance.

"Don't do my friend like that. She got her own money!" Careesha spat while slapping his shoulder playfully. "We're about to get ready though. Give me about forty minutes at most," she said before jogging back to her apartment.

Tory had just applied a legendary amount of pressure behind her little ass. There was no way she could turn him down. A nigga that could move mountains had always turned her on, but a nigga willing to move mountains in her name was a whole ass dream come true, one of the biggest flexes in her book.

Chapter 35

Murk surprised everyone with his quick transition into legitimacy. Upon his return, he decided that it was time he graduated from the streets. It was a child's playground these days, so he passed the torch to Glock Gang. They handled all the heavy-duty dirty business in the streets now. They were the new Black Ops team for Rock Nation, ready and willing to do any job that involved bullets, blood, and gun smoke.

Murk had bigger plans for the Vultures though. Now that J-Rock was out of the picture, he was one hundred percent his own boss and could literally do as he pleased. After a week of sitting around and a long talk with Swiss at the county jail visitation, he decided to take Ronnie up on his longtime standing offer.

Every time Murk and his crew would visit the training facility, Ronnie tried to convince them to sign onto the private security franchise. It was only one of their many business but paid a lot of the bills. Ronnie felt like they were perfect fits for the private sector because of their natural fearlessness and new tactical skills.

It was good legit money, so his Vultures would be able to feed their families without risking facing life in prison. Murk agreed to sign on with Ronnie for two years before branching off and starting his own private security business under the franchise. He would learn plenty of skills and rake up tons of business experience from the opportunity, so it was a no-brainer.

Lately, he'd been able to breathe easier knowing he didn't have to risk his life on the daily. They didn't even carry unregistered guns anymore. Everything was company-owned, from the cars to the guns, so they couldn't be fucked with. Ronnie and his brother were openly feared by the government, so their company name held major weight.

It was an off day for Murk though. He waited patiently at Static Lounge for his date. She insisted that he show up by himself, so Murk sat there in a public place without security for the first time in a *long* time. Usually, that would've been an enormous red flag for him, but he literally trusted this woman with his heartbeat, so he respected her wishes. Plus, he was actually safer with her than any of his Vultures. Even Ronnie himself.

Isabella walked up to his VIP section and stopped at the red rope that closed the section off. "May I enter?" she asked sweetly, gaining his full attention.

He looked up with wide eyes of pure satisfaction. It was his first time seeing her dressed all the way up. She was in combat training gear most of the time, and seeing her in the dress and heels, Murk couldn't understand. She looked like a supermodel easily.

"Damn, my bad!" he said before popping up and removing the rope, so she could enter the booth. "You smell and look good, girl. I ain't even going to lie. You could've been a damn supermodel."

"I make three times as much as the richest models… You clean up nice yourself though," she complimented with a smile as she sat down. She liked how he looked with his jewelry and Burberry button down.

"I step out when I want to," he assured while giving her a seductive stare after taking a seat across from her.

She looked around, purposely avoiding that toxic eye contact he was giving her. "This is a decent place right here. Laney owns it?"

"Yeah, she's a part owner now. She used to manage it, but she a housewife these days," he informed.

"Okayyy, that's nice for her... I see you went all out on the drinks," she pointed out. Multiple bottles of liquor, wine, and champaign set on the table in big ice buckets.

"Yup! You see I'm drinking out the bottle," he said before grabbing a cold champagne bottle in his right hand. "Nah, I didn't know what you wanted to drink, so I got a little bit of everything."

She nodded her approval. "I like that. I came for a good time, so let's get to it," she encouraged before reaching forward and grabbing a bottle of champagne for herself.

****

Three hours later, they ended up at Murk's new apartment downtown. He moved out of the place he shared with his baby mother for obvious reasons and set up a healthy joint-custody schedule for his daughter. He tried to make it work with his baby mother, but she just wasn't it for him, so he ended up with his current bachelor's pad.

They didn't waste any time. They barely made it up to Murk's floor on the elevator before they ripped each other's clothes off. They were both full of alcohol and lust. Their physical attraction was highly vibrant, and they were both currently lost in each other.

Isabella was a unique ass woman, and Murk was extremely turned on by her. It showed too by the way he caressed her body with his hands. The fact that he was delicate and firm with it had her turned on. He was a unique man in her eyes and had more potential than he gave himself credit for. Those thoughts were in their minds as they made out on the couch, but no words were said. They were vibing on a totally different level, so no words were really needed at the moment.

She suddenly pulled away from him, reached for her clutch purse, and pulled out a single Magnum condom for him. She tossed it on his lap before standing up slowly and sexily. She kept eye contact with him as she slid out of her dress seductively. It was stretchy, so she didn't have to do too much to get out of it.

It didn't take Murk any time to get out of his pants and slide the condom on. His dick was already rock hard, and he was ready to get inside of her. He'd been so caught up in business lately that he hadn't had any pussy in almost two months.

He outstretched his arms, reaching for her while biting his lip. She bit her own lip as she closed the distance between them and sat down on his curved dick slowly.

They both gyrated slowly as he made himself comfortable in her tight hole. It was clear she wasn't getting stretched on a regular basis. She was a busy muthafucka her damn self, and most men around her parts were terrified of her.

He held her closer as they sped up, and he began to bounce her up and down on his dick. She didn't have the fattest booty, but she was slim-thick and had a good amount of cheeks for her body build. Then, her little ass cheeks were soft and loose on top of that, so he enjoyed the view as he looked down over her and saw her cheeks clapping on his dick.

Little did he know, she'd been celibate for the past five years. She rubbed her slit every once in a while, but she hadn't been penetrated in years. So, although his dick was barely average sized, it still did her some damage. It was not even three minutes in, and she was shaking on top of him as she climaxed. She went limp for a few seconds with her eyes rolled to the back of her head.

"If you don't cum before me this second time, you're going to be ass out of luck," she warned before hopping off of him and getting back on the couch on all fours beside him.

"Alright, bet!" he agreed before standing up and getting behind her.

He bent down to take a good close look at her spread pussy from behind and nodded his approval before standing back up and sliding back inside of her. He wrapped his left hand around her long hair twice and went to work. The view was ten times better from behind.

The bitch was the definition of sexy, and her pussy was watery. It didn't take long for Murk to cum, and Isabella was right in sync with his ass. They both enjoyed the ecstasy for a few moments before getting cleaned up and dressed.

"You staying the night?" he asked hopefully.

That was not something he usually did, but obviously rules didn't apply with Isabella. The fact that she was in his man cave said it all. And the face that she gave him in response to his question said some more.

"Damn, why you got to look like that?" he asked with a twisted face to match hers.

She was still standing, fixing herself up. "Because I don't do that, Murk. I don't even do what we just did, but I laid with you because you're different like me, and I like you. I really enjoyed myself with you tonight, and I'm not opposed to doing this again, but I don't want you to get the wrong idea."

"That's cool. I'm not tripping," he responded nonchalantly although he was really slightly disappointed.

"I hope you're not," she said while picking up her clutch off the table and turning back toward him. "Listen, I love that you graduated from the petty street life. Keep pushing yourself in training and take the security profession serious. J-Rock's gone now. It's time for you to shine, cutie," she encouraged before blowing him a sweet kiss and letting herself out of his apartment.

Murk didn't speak. He just let her leave. He wanted to grab her, and kiss her, and convince her to stay in the US, so she'd be closer to him, but he pushed that shit down. He had to just enjoy her in the way that he could. Plus, like she said, he needed to focus. A relationship wasn't what he needed right then.

He was currently going through official military Black Ops basic training and had three phases of advanced training afterward. He was also still adjusting to being on the right side of the law. For the first time in forever, he wasn't involved in criminal activity, and it felt weird to him still.

He didn't know what else to do with himself, so he laid there and reflected on all he'd been through in those streets. It was a miracle he made it out.

Chapter 36

Two months later, Zion's fight was finally present. It was the fight boxing fans all around the globe had been anticipating, the battle for the title of light-heavyweight champion of the world. Majority of the fans were against Zion, and Zion wasn't fazed by that at all.

He knew that they were scared to go against Emmanuel Sanchez. They knew exactly what he was capable of, but they had no idea what Zion was really made of. They had only seen old fights and recent training clips of Zion. They hadn't seen him in action recently, and that was why Zion was a huge underdog.

It was the day before the fight, and Zion was in Vegas already. He got there seventy-two hours ago and had been holed in the gym ever since. He would leave the training gym and go straight to the arena to fight. He was locked in.

"You see how much better you've been doing the past few days. That's because you've been locked in and fully focused. Now, had you would've brought your ass to Nevada when I told you two months ago, you would've been way more locked in," his head coach blabbered at him as he took a brief break in the corner of the ring.

Zion gave the old man a knowing look. "We not going to do that, OG. I'm locked in right now, and that's all that matters. I'm just ready for tomorrow."

"Me as well, but I just need you to keep your temper in check, and the fight should be over quickly. You better knock him out fast because the man definitely has you beat in the stamina field. You're a better fighter, I believe, but he has more energy, so you have to protect your strength. The only way you're going to do that is to knock him out before you get tired because if you don't, shit's going to get ugly for you, son."

Zion took the advice to the chin. He didn't like to believe — or admit — that any man was better than him at anything, but his coach was right. Emmanuel could run nearly twenty miles straight without hydration. Zion could barely run ten with hydration. It was his only disadvantage, so his fighting skills would have to make up for it. "We'll see what that nigga made of tomorrow."

"Yes, indeed. Now, get your ass back in that ring!" Coach yelled in his drill sergeant voice.

Zion popped up and bounced his way back into the ring to greet his sparring partner before catching him with a quick jab and taking two quick steps back.

****

"Everything's on the line in this fight. You either leave a zero or a hero. This is not fun, and we're not about to play a game. This is a deadly sport with millions on the line. Go in that ring with your lion's eyes and lock in on your prey. You're from the nasty street on the westside of Charlotte. Show all these muthafuckas what you're made of!" Coach preached ferociously into Zion's ear.

Zion focused on his breathing and locked in on his prey like Coach said. He was staring dead at Emmanuel, and Emmanuel stared dead back. Neither of them broke eye contact either. They weren't distracted by the twenty thousand people in attendance at the Sphere Arena that they were in, and they definitely weren't fazed by the millions of people who were watching on TV. They were the only two people in the world at the moment.

They were called to the center of the ring, touched gloves, and that legendary bell rang. It was that time that everyone had been waiting for, and Zion's pride immediately drove him to take the cocky route.

"What's up, bruh?" Zion asked casually. "I just wanted to say I'm sorry for all that shit I said about your daddy in my last interview," he apologized after slipping two jabs that Emmanuel threw.

"I'm going to send you to the hospital with a broken face while I tell the world about this conversation," Emmanuel said before faking a left and catching Zion with a sturdy right hook.

"Ahhh, there we go! I like that!" Zion spat with a smile. "I eat those like fish and grits."

"Eat this!" Emmanuel spat before sending a mean combination of jabs and hooks.

Zion blocked two punches, sidestepped, and caught Emmanuel with a solid hook of his own. "That jaw weak, boy! I'll break your face before you break mines! Believe that!"

Emmanuel's coach yelled at him to stop talking, and he immediately silenced himself. Zion could tell he had gotten to Emmanuel by the look in his eyes. He was trying to really hurt Zion and make an example out of him. He hit Zion with a hook and tried to follow with another hook, but Zion was quicker and caught Emmanuel with a counter hook that had him stumbling.

"This what I do, nigga!" Zion spat cheerfully as he allowed Emmanuel a moment to get right.

The crowd erupted a little after that punch, and it juiced Zion up. It was time to show the world what he was made of. He went on the offense once Emmanuel put his gloves back up. He raised a nasty combo down on Emmanuel and landed a few blows before the bell rang. It was the end of the first round, and it looked good for him.

Chapter 37

Laney was front and center, watching her man's fight proudly. She had Mini, Ta'Jae, Tory, and Lester sitting alongside her. She appeared to be unfazed, but that was just for the cameras. In all honesty, she was just as nervous as she was when she watched him fight in that death tournament.

"Let's ride, nigga! You a westside baby! Show 'em wassup!" Tory yelled out with cupped hands over his mouth like it was going to make Zion hear him any better.

"Ma, I'm scared. You think Daddy gon' beat him?" Mini leaned in and asked Laney after Zion was hit with a mean uppercut. It sent him stumbling this time.

Laney put a reassuring hand on Mini's leg. "He's going to knock that man the fuck out, baby. Don't be scared. Your daddy is the toughest nigga I know, and that's saying *a lot*.

"You got this, babyyyyyy!" Laney screamed at the top of her lungs, making sure that Zion heard her encouragement.

Zion quickly shook the uppercut off and got back in the fight. They went at it like two male lions in the same cage. Zion landed blows on Emmanuel, and Emmanuel landed blows on Zion.

It was nearing the end of the third round when Emmanuel had a boost of energy and came at Zion like Sonic. He caught Zion in the corner and hit him with a combo so mean that it ended with another uppercut, but this one dropped Zion like a tree leaf in the fall.

The crowd erupted thunderously as the referee began the countdown over Zion, who struggled to get up onto his feet.

"Nooooo! Get up, Daddyyyy!" Mini screamed frantically with tears in her eyes.

Mini's tears activated Laney's. "Get up, baby! Get upppp!"

"Hold on!" Lester spat. "He's good! He's getting up."

To the crowd's surprise, Zion got back to his feet and was checked out. He was ready to fight again. The bell rang again, and they finished the last twelve seconds in the round before heading into their corners for their break.

"Boy, that nigga can't scare me like that. I got way too much money riding on this game!" Tory said.

Laney gave him a twisted look of pure disgust. "Bitch ass nigga, ain't nobody make you bet on my man. If you ain't got nothing good to say, shut the fuck up!" she spat with more force than she knew she had.

Tory looked at her with wide eyes. "Damn, killer! My bad! Shittt."

"Zion doing bad up there, so you could understand why she's frustrated. You could've left that comment to yourself, youngin. Have some sympathy. The stakes are high for all of us," Lester told Tory.

Tory nodded understandably. "I ain't mean no disrespect, Boss Lady."

"Tory, please! Not right now!" Laney warned before clenching her teeth and her asshole as the bell rang, signaling the start of the fourth round.

Chapter 38

Zion was furious. He had just gotten knocked out in front of millions of people, and Emmanuel was dancing while he was on the ground. There were no more smiles from him or playful remarks. He meant business and had fire in his eyes. He was done playing with that taco eating muthafucka.

"I know your jaw's feeling a little loose after that uppercut. Your ass was out cold for a few seconds there," Emmanuel teased as they danced around the center of the ring, trying to find openings. "I'm about to put you in a coma this time!"

Zion didn't respond. He was in his zone. He wanted to unleash a can of whoop ass on Emmanuel but was careful not to tire himself out.

"I'm really glad you got up, homie," Emmanuel said after throwing two quick jabs that Zion blocked even quicker.

Zion made sure to study Emmanuel's body movements as they exchanged small blows. He went in for another knockout, and Zion caught him in the ribs. He still didn't gloat, but he could see that Emmanuel felt the hell out of that hook. That was what he needed.

"That was alright. Let's see what you made out of because I can take a punch, homie!" Emmanuel bragged before rushing Zion back into the corner.

It was like he did a few lines of meth by the way he was on Zion's ass. He hit Zion with a few super-combinations of punches, and Zion threw some back when he could, but he spent most of the time trying to block Emmanuel's assault.

He took a deep breath and used his gloves to push Emmanuel back three steps. Instead of using the opportunity to dart out of the corner like most fighters would've done, Zion stayed put and waved for Emmanuel to come back.

Zion's coach yelled at him from the side, telling him to get out of the corner, but Zion wasn't trying to hear that shit. Emmanuel charged him again and rained more punches down on him. Zion took a few blows before catching Emmanuel with a stiff jab that sent him stumbling back.

"Get on his ass!" his coach instructed from the top of his old, raspy lungs.

Zion listened to the coach this time and got on Emmanuel's ass. He hit him with two more jabs with his right hand, a left hook, followed by a nasty uppercut that sent Emmanuel backwards, off of his feet. Zion literally put everything he had into that uppercut, and it felt good to see it connect so wonderfully.

The crowd was in shock. Most people were quiet as the referee counted down over Emmanuel. All that could be heard in that vicinity was Zion's people cheering proudly for him.

"7... 8... 9... 10!" The bell rang, and Zion's team rushed into the ring to congratulate him.

He won the fight in four rounds and was now the light heavyweight champion of the world. He was also twenty-five million dollars richer, and it felt good as hell.

After the announcer announced the winner, a pretty blonde reporter for ESPN asked Zion for a quick interview, and he obliged. He answered all of her questions simply, but when she asked him what he thought about Emmanuel, he said this; "He's definitely a warrior and the best fighter I've ever had the pleasure of getting in the ring with. I'm honored to win this fight tonight, and I want to make it clear that he has my respect as a boxer. Definitely one of the greats for sure."

He walked out of the ring after the interview and found his family immediately. He needed them at the moment just as much as they needed him.

****

Back in the locker room, Laney and Mini were huddled around Zion as he caught his breath. "Y'all do know I heard y'all asses yelling while I was in the ring, right?"

Mini smiled. "Laney was crying, but I was trying to tell her everything was going to be just fine."

Laney's mouth dropped in pure shock. "That lil' heffa is lying through her teeth! She was scared you were going to lose, and I let her know that you were the toughest nigga I know."

"Oh, yeahhh?" he asked before shooting a playful jab to Mini's jaw. "Go wait outside with Lester. Let me holla at yo' mama for a few."

"Okay, that's cool. I'm about to go make some content in the ring anyway," Mini informed before standing up and walking out.

"Take Lester with you," Laney shouted behind her before turning toward her man. "What's up, Zaddy?" He motioned for her to pull her chair closer to him, and she quickly followed directions. "What's up, baby? What's on your mind?"

"We finally made it, baby!" he said as he finally allowed the tears to escape his eyes. "I'm out of prison, and you out the streets. We got a beautiful family and a wonderful future ahead of us. I just been sitting here, thanking God, over and over. I just want you to know how a nigga feeling right now."

"Awwwwwwww, my babyyyyyy!" she said before dropping tears of her own.

She got up out of her chair and sat on his lap. When she wrapped her arms around him, he cried real pure tears of joy for the very first time ever in his life. Before this, he'd only ever shed tears of pain.

He squeezed her tightly as he sobbed uncontrollably. He was showing her that she was his safe place, and the feeling overwhelmed her. She broke down with him, and they cried in each other's arms. It was a sacred moment that they were sharing.

"God is good, babe. He got big plans for us. This only the beginning," she assured while wiping the tears from her face.

Lock Down Publications and Ca$h Presents Assisted Publishing Packages

Due to an increase in the price of services we have increased our prices. The prices below reflect the price increase as of 11/1/24.

BASIC PACKAGE $699 Editing Cover Design Formatting	UPGRADED PACKAGE $1000 Typing Editing Cover Design Formatting Upload eBooks to Amazon Upload Paperback to Amazon
ADVANCE PACKAGE $1,400 Typing Editing (line editing/content) Cover Design Formatting Copyright Registration Proofreading Upload eBooks to Amazon Upload Paperback to Amazon	LDP SUPREME PACKAGE $1,700 Typing Editing (line editing/content) Cover Design Formatting Copyright Registration Proofreading Set up Amazon Account Upload eBooks to Amazon Upload Paperback to Amazon Advertise on LDP's Amazon and Facebook Page

***Other services available upon request.
Additional charges may apply

Lock Down Publications
P.O. Box 944
Stockbridge, GA 30281-9998
Phone: 470 303-9761
Email: lockdownpublications@gmail.com

163

Submission Guideline

Submit the first three chapters of your completed manuscript to ldpsubmissions@gmail.com. In the subject line add **Your Book's Title**. The manuscript must be in a Word Doc file and sent as an attachment. Document should be in Times New Roman, double spaced, and in size 12 font. Also, provide your synopsis and full contact information. If sending multiple submissions, they must each be in a separate email.

Have a story but no way to send it electronically? You can still submit to LDP/Ca$h Presents. Send in the first three chapters, written or typed, of your completed manuscript to:

LDP: Submissions Dept
P.O. Box 944
Stockbridge, GA 30281-9998

DO NOT send original manuscript. Must be a duplicate.
Provide your synopsis and a cover letter containing your full contact information.

Thanks for considering LDP and Ca$h Presents.

NEW RELEASES

BLOODLINE OF A SAVAGE 1,2&3
THESE VICIOUS STREETS 1,2&3
RELENTLESS GOON
RELENTLESS GOON 2
BY PRINCE A. TAUHID

THE BUTTERFLY MAFIA 1-3
BY FUMIYA PAYNE

A THUG'S STREET PRINCESS 1,2&3
BY MEESHA

CITY OF SMOKE 1& 2
BY MOLOTTI

STEPPERS 1,2&3
THE REAL BADDIES OF CHI-RAQ
BY KING RIO

THE LANE 1&2
BY KEN-KEN SPENCE

THUG OF SPADES 1,2&3
LOVE IN THE TRENCHES 2
CORNER BOY CHRONICLES
BY COREY ROBINSON

TIL DEATH 3
BY ARYANNA

THE BIRTH OF A GANGSTER 4
BY DELMONT PLAYER

PRODUCT OF THE STREETS 1&2
BY DEMOND "MONEY" ANDERSON

NO TIME FOR ERROR
BY KEESE

MONEY HUNGRY DEMONS 1,2&3
BY TRANAY ADAMS

HUNGRY FOR MONEY 1&2
BY SLIMBOS

A THUGGISH PASSION
KILLAZ ON STANDBY 1&2
LAND OF DA HOOLIGANZ 1,2&3
FRESH OFF DA PORCH
BY IRA B.

COUNTDOWN OF A KILLA 1&2
GUNS DOWN, BOTTOMS UP 1&2
SEX, MURDA AND GOD
BY LO-LIFE

THE LEVEL UP 1&2
BY LUXURY KING

FO'EVA ROLLIN' 1&2
BY ASSA RAYMOND BAKER

HUB CITY MENACE 1&2
BY J. WHITE

KILLA CREW
DYING FOR LIKES
BY ARYANNA

IF YOU CROSS ME ONCE 6
ANGEL 5
By Anthony Fields

IMMA DIE BOUT MINE 5
By Aryanna

A THUGS STREET PRINCESS 3
EMBRACING THE LOVE OF A BOSS
By Meesha

PRODUCT OF THE STREETS 3
By Demond Money Anderson

STANDING ON HER BUSINESS
BY DG SANTANA

GET IT IN SLUGS 1&2
B. STALLS

CORNER BOYS 2
By Corey Robinson

THE MURDER QUEENS 6&7
By Michael Gallon

CITY OF SMOKE 3
By Molotti

CONFESSIONS OF A DOPEBOY
By Nicholas Lock

TENDER
BY KHUFU

THA TAKEOVER
By Keith Chandler

BETRAYAL OF A G 2
By Ray Vinci

CRIME BOSS 4
By Playa Ray

Coming Soon from Lock Down Publications/Ca$h Presents

RAN OFF ON THE PLUG 2 by **PAPER BOI RARI**
STREET REDEMPTION by **TONY DANIELS**
SAVAGE FAMILY EMPIRE by **PRINCE TAUHID**
BAD BITCHES WIT' GUNZ by **DIESEL**
THE SINGLE LADIES by **DIESEL**
COKE BY THE TRUCKLOAD by **DIESEL**
PROBLEM SOLVED by **DIESEL**
TIPPIN' THE SCALES by **DIESEL**
OPPS CRY TOO by **SAYNOMORE**
A GANGSTA'S KARMA by **FLAME**

AVAILABLE NOW

RESTRAINING ORDER 1 & 2
By **CA$H & Coffee**

LOVE KNOWS NO BOUNDARIES 1-3
By **Coffee**

RAISED AS A GOON I, II, III & IV
BRED BY THE SLUMS I, II, III
BLAST FOR ME I & II
ROTTEN TO THE CORE I II III
A BRONX TALE I, II, III
DUFFLE BAG CARTEL I II III IV V VI
HEARTLESS GOON I II III IV V
A SAVAGE DOPEBOY I II
DRUG LORDS I II III
CUTTHROAT MAFIA I II
KING OF THE TRENCHES
By **Ghost**

LAY IT DOWN I & II
LAST OF A DYING BREED I II
BLOOD STAINS OF A SHOTTA I & II III
By **Jamaica**

LOYAL TO THE GAME I II III
LIFE OF SIN I, II III
By **TJ & Jelissa**

IF LOVING HIM IS WRONG…I & II
LOVE ME EVEN WHEN IT HURTS I II III
By **Jelissa**

PUSH IT TO THE LIMIT
By **Bre' Hayes**

BLOODY COMMAS I & II
SKI MASK CARTEL I, II & III
KING OF NEW YORK I II, III IV V
RISE TO POWER I II III
COKE KINGS I II III IV V
BORN HEARTLESS I II III IV
KING OF THE TRAP I II
By **T.J. Edwards**

WHEN THE STREETS CLAP BACK I & II III
THE HEART OF A SAVAGE I II III IV
MONEY MAFIA I II
LOYAL TO THE SOIL I II III
By **Jibril Williams**

A DISTINGUISHED THUG STOLE MY HEART I - III
LOVE SHOULDN'T HURT I II III IV
RENEGADE BOYS 1-4
PAID IN KARMA 1-3
SAVAGE STORMS 1-3
AN UNFORESEEN LOVE 1-3
BABY, I'M WINTERTIME COLD 1-3
A THUG'S STREET PRINCESS 1&2
By **Meesha**

CUM FOR ME 1-8
An LDP Erotica Collaboration

BLOOD OF A BOSS 1-5
SHADOWS OF THE GAME
TRAP BASTARD
By **Askari**

A GANGSTER'S CODE 1-3
A GANGSTER'S SYN 1-3
THE SAVAGE LIFE 1-3
CHAINED TO THE STREETS 1-3
BLOOD ON THE MONEY 1-3
A GANGSTA'S PAIN 1-3
BEAUTIFUL LIES AND UGLY TRUTHS
CHURCH IN THESE STREETS
By **J-Blunt**

THE STREETS BLEED MURDER 1-3
THE HEART OF A GANGSTA 1-3
By **Jerry Jackson**

WHEN A GOOD GIRL GOES BAD
By **Adrienne**

THE COST OF LOYALTY 1-3
By **Kweli**

BRIDE OF A HUSTLA 1-3
THE FETTI GIRLS 1-3
CORRUPTED BY A GANGSTA 1-4
BLINDED BY HIS LOVE
THE PRICE YOU PAY FOR LOVE 1-3
DOPE GIRL MAGIC 1-3
By **Destiny Skai**

A KINGPIN'S AMBITION
A KINGPIN'S AMBITION II
I MURDER FOR THE DOUGH
By **Ambitious**

A DOPEBOY'S PRAYER
By **Eddie "Wolf" Lee**

TRUE SAVAGE 1-7
DOPE BOY MAGIC 1-3
MIDNIGHT CARTEL 1-3
CITY OF KINGZ 1&2
NIGHTMARE ON SILENT AVE
THE PLUG OF LIL MEXICO 1&2
CLASSIC CITY
By **Chris Green**

LOVE & CHASIN' PAPER
By **Qay Crockett**

THE KING CARTEL 1-3
By **Frank Gresham**

THESE NIGGAS AIN'T LOYAL 1-3
By **Nikki Tee**

GANGSTA SHYT 1-3
By **CATO**

THE ULTIMATE BETRAYAL
By **Phoenix**

BOSS'N UP 1-3
By **Royal Nicole**

I LOVE YOU TO DEATH
By **Destiny J**

BROOKLYN HUSTLAZ
By **Boogsy Morina**

GANGSTA CITY
By **Teddy Duke**

TO DIE IN VAIN
SINS OF A HUSTLA
By **ASAD**

I RIDE FOR MY HITTA
I STILL RIDE FOR MY HITTA
By **Misty Holt**

A GANGSTER'S REVENGE 1-4
THE BOSS MAN'S DAUGHTERS 1-5
A SAVAGE LOVE 1&2
BAE BELONGS TO ME 1&2
A HUSTLER'S DECEIT 1-3
WHAT BAD BITCHES DO 1-3
SOUL OF A MONSTER 1-3
KILL ZONE
A DOPE BOY'S QUEEN 1-3
TIL DEATH 1-3
IMMA DIE BOUT MINE 1-5
By **Aryanna**

BROOKLYN ON LOCK 1 & 2
By **Sonovia**

A DRUG KING AND HIS DIAMOND 1-3
A DOPEMAN'S RICHES
HER MAN, MINE'S TOO 1&2
CASH MONEY HO'S
THE WIFEY I USED TO BE 1&2
PRETTY GIRLS DO NASTY THINGS
By **Nicole Goosby**

THE STREETS ARE CALLING
By **Duquie Wilson**

LIPSTICK KILLAH 1-3
CRIME OF PASSION 1-3
FRIEND OR FOE 1-3
By **Mimi**

TRAPHOUSE KING 1-3
KINGPIN KILLAZ 1-3
STREET KINGS 1&2
PAID IN BLOOD 1&2
CARTEL KILLAZ 1-3
DOPE GODS 1&2
By **Hood Rich**

STEADY MOBBN' 1-3
THE STREETS STAINED MY SOUL 1-3
By **Marcellus Allen**

WHO SHOT YA 1-3
SON OF A DOPE FIEND 1-4
HEAVEN GOT A GHETTO 1&2
SKI MASK MONEY 1&2
By **Renta**

GORILLAZ IN THE BAY 1-4
TEARS OF A GANGSTA 1/&2
3X KRAZY 1&2
STRAIGHT BEAST MODE 1&2
By **DE'KARI**

TRIGGADALE 1-3
MURDA WAS THE CASE 1-3
By **Elijah R. Freeman**

MARRIED TO A BOSS 1-3
By **Destiny Skai & Chris Green**

SLAUGHTER GANG 1-3
RUTHLESS HEART 1-3
By **Willie Slaughter**

GOD BLESS THE TRAPPERS 1-3
THESE SCANDALOUS STREETS 1-3
FEAR MY GANGSTA 1-5
THESE STREETS DON'T LOVE NOBODY 1-2
BURY ME A G 1-5
A GANGSTA'S EMPIRE 1-4
THE DOPEMAN'S BODYGAURD 1&2
THE REALEST KILLAZ 1-3
THE LAST OF THE OGS 1-3
By **Tranay Adams**

KINGZ OF THE GAME 1-7
CRIME BOSS 1-4
By **Playa Ray**

FUK SHYT
By **Blakk Diamond**

DON'T F#CK WITH MY HEART 1&2
By **Linnea**

ADDICTED TO THE DRAMA 1-3
IN THE ARM OF HIS BOSS
By **Jamila**

LOYALTY AIN'T PROMISED 1&2
By **Keith Williams**

FOREVER GANGSTA 1&2
GLOCKS ON SATIN SHEETS 1&2
By **Adrian Dulan**

YAYO 1-4
A SHOOTER'S AMBITION 1&2
BRED IN THE GAME
By **S. Allen**

TRAP GOD 1-3
RICH $AVAGE 1-3
MONEY IN THE GRAVE 1-3
CARTEL MONEY
By **Martell Troublesome Bolden**

TOE TAGZ 1-4
LEVELS TO THIS SHYT 1&2
IT'S JUST ME AND YOU
By **Ah'Million**

KINGPIN DREAMS 1-3
RAN OFF ON DA PLUG
By **Paper Boi Rari**

THE STREETS MADE ME 1-3
By **Larry D. Wright**

CONFESSIONS OF A GANGSTA 1-4
CONFESSIONS OF A JACKBOY 1-3
CONFESSIONS OF A HITMAN
By **Nicholas Lock**

I'M NOTHING WITHOUT HIS LOVE
SINS OF A THUG
TO THE THUG I LOVED BEFORE
A GANGSTA SAVED XMAS
IN A HUSTLER I TRUST
By **Monet Dragun**

QUIET MONEY 1-3
THUG LIFE 1-3
EXTENDED CLIP 1&2
A GANGSTA'S PARADISE
By **Trai'Quan**

CAUGHT UP IN THE LIFE 1-3
THE STREETS NEVER LET GO 1-3
By **Robert Baptiste**

NEW TO THE GAME 1-3
MONEY, MURDER & MEMORIES 1-3
By **Malik D. Rice**

THE LIFE OF A HOOD STAR
By **Ca$h & Rashia Wilson**

THE STREETS WILL NEVER CLOSE 1-4
By **K'ajji**

LIFE OF A SAVAGE 1-4
A GANGSTA'S QUR'AN 1-4
MURDA SEASON 1-3
GANGLAND CARTEL 1-3
CHI'RAQ GANGSTAS 1-4
KILLERS ON ELM STREET 1-3
JACK BOYZ N DA BRONX 1-3
A DOPEBOY'S DREAM 1-3
JACK BOYS VS DOPE BOYS 1-3
COKE GIRLZ
COKE BOYS
SOSA GANG 1&2
BRONX SAVAGES
BODYMORE KINGPINS
BLOOD OF A GOON
By **Romell Tukes**

CREAM 2-3
THE STREETS WILL TALK
By **Yolanda Moore**

CONCRETE KILLA 1-3
VICIOUS LOYALTY 1-3
By **Kingpen**

THE ULTIMATE SACRIFICE 1-6
KHADIFI
IF YOU CROSS ME ONCE 1-5
ANGEL 1-4
IN THE BLINK OF AN EYE
By **Anthony Fields**

NIGHTMARES OF A HUSTLA 1-3
BLOOD AND GAMES 1&2
By **King Dream**

HARD AND RUTHLESS 1&2
MOB TOWN 251
THE BILLIONAIRE BENTLEYS 1-3
REAL G'S MOVE IN SILENCE
By **Von Diesel**

MOB TIES 1-7
SOUL OF A HUSTLER, HEART OF A KILLER 1-3
GORILLAZ IN THE TRENCHES
By **SayNoMore**

BODYMORE MURDERLAND 1-3
THE BIRTH OF A GANGSTER 1-4
By **Delmont Player**

FOR THE LOVE OF A BOSS 1&2
By **C. D. Blue**

KILLA KOUNTY 1-5
By **Khufu**

MOBBED UP 1-4
THE BRICK MAN 1-5
THE COCAINE PRINCESS 1-10
STEPPERS 1-3
SUPER GREMLIN 1-4
By **King Rio**

MONEY GAME 1&2
By **Smoove Dolla**

A GANGSTA'S KARMA 1-4
By **FLAME**

KING OF THE TRENCHES 1-3
By **GHOST & TRANAY ADAMS**

QUEEN OF THE ZOO 1&2
By **Black Migo**

GRIMEY WAYS 1-3
BETRAYAL OF A G
By **Ray Vinci**

XMAS WITH AN ATL SHOOTER
By **Ca$h & Destiny Skai**

KING KILLA 1&2
By **Vincent "Vitto" Holloway**

BETRAYAL OF A THUG 1&2
By **Fre$h**

THE MURDER QUEENS 1-6
By **Michael Gallon**

FOR THE LOVE OF BLOOD 1-4
By **Jamel Mitchell**

HOOD CONSIGLIERE 1&2
NO TIME FOR ERROR
By **Keese**

PROTÉGÉ OF A LEGEND 1&2
LOVE IN THE TRENCHES 1&2
By **Corey Robinson**

THE PLUG'S RUTHLESS DAUGHTER 1&2
By **Tony Daniels**

BORN IN THE GRAVE 1-3
CRIME PAYS 1&2
By **Self Made Tay**

MOAN IN MY MOUTH
By **XTASY**

TORN BETWEEN A GANGSTER AND A
GENTLEMAN
By **J-BLUNT & Miss Kim**

HERE TODAY GONE TOMORROW 1&2
By **Fly Rock**

PILLOW PRINCESS
By **S. Hawkins**

SANCTIFIED AND HORNY
by **XTASY**

WOMEN LIE MEN LIE 1-4
FIFTY SHADES OF SNOW 1-3
STACK BEFORE YOU SPLURGE
GIRLS FALL LIKE DOMINOES
NAÏVE TO THE STREETS
By **ROY MILLIGAN**

LOYALTY IS EVERYTHING 1-3
CITY OF SMOKE 1&2
By **Molotti**

THE BUTTERFLY MAFIA 1-4
SALUTE MY SAVAGERY 1&2
By **Fumiya Payne**

THE LANE 1&2
By **Ken-Ken Spence**

THE PUSSY TRAP 1-5
By **Nene Capri**

DIRTY DNA
By **Blaque**

BOOKS BY LDP'S CEO, CA$H

TRUST IN NO MAN
TRUST IN NO MAN 2
TRUST IN NO MAN 3
BONDED BY BLOOD
SHORTY GOT A THUG
THUGS CRY
THUGS CRY 2
THUGS CRY 3
TRUST NO BITCH
TRUST NO BITCH 2
TRUST NO BITCH 3
TIL MY CASKET DROPS
RESTRAINING ORDER
RESTRAINING ORDER 2
IN LOVE WITH A CONVICT
LIFE OF A HOOD STAR
XMAS WITH AN ATL SHOOTER